THE JADE PAGODA

BETTY HALE HYATT

ROBERT HALE · LONDON

ISBN 0 7091 9372 6

Robert Hale Limited,
Clerkenwell House,
Clerkenwell Green,
London EC1R 0HT

Printed in Great Britain by
St Edmundsbury Press, Bury St Edmunds, Suffolk.
Bound by Weatherby Woolnough.

*For Martin
and a time in
Kashmir*

THE
JADE PAGODA

expectedly he raised his fist; in an unusual burst of fierce courage and bravado, he shook it at the bandit chief, who sat unmoving on his horse, the high fur hat covering the bald head like a crown.

Without another word and not wasting another moment on the angry bandits, he turned and strode down the rocky path into the trees, his back very straight and tall, to where he'd flung the packs we had removed in those last hectic moments from our ponies and yaks we'd had to leave on the other side.

I stumbled after him, so weary I could hardly lift my feet, but, realizing his strength and seeing the way he walked with abandoned care for what might have been and for what lay ahead of us, I found an extra measure of strength to go on to that promised safety.

Chanda was folded on the ground where she had sunk with her precious burden when we reached this side of the bridge. I marveled at her endurance even with the baby, as she had shown on this traumatic flight, and to be calm in the face of jeopardy no matter what it entailed.

Jaseen picked up the smallest of the packs and hoisted it onto my back, adjusting it with deft sure fingers so that I could carry it easily. Then he swung the other, far more heavy pack on his strong young shoulders, saying nothing because we had very little time. With a glance at Chanda, then at me, he turned and took off down the mountain.

I waited until Chanda shifted herself and rose to her feet, the loose woolen burnoose falling in deep folds about her soft leather boots, and I peeked at the baby she carried in a fold of woolen shawl strapped firmly to her back. He was asleep, and I silently thanked God that he was so well adjusted as to do so even during the worst of times. I thought Bianca would have been proud of her little son, as well as the loyal nursemaid who had given him his life's milk from her own full breasts. Chanda picked up the bundle tied in a shawl, and walked ahead of me in our descent of the wild Himalayan mountainside. Jaseen was already lost in the trees around a bend in the trail. I followed slowly, apprehensively, for I could not dismiss Khan Shayet so easily.

It was still light of day when we reached the ancient gompa, a Tibetan Lamaist monastery, its walls red in the last rays of the dying sun. The old chortens, those strange dry stone stupas which held dead lamas, were clustered around its base in deep shadows, but the steps leading up to the gompa were in sudden relief of light and shadow as if to guide us up to the thick double gate, which was closed.

During the last frantic months, I had learned to accept the monasteries in the remote mountains as safe refuges from all the elements as well as from my enemy. The gompas of Ladakh, Tibet and Nepal were protection for every pilgrim caught out in the Himalayas, and pilgrims were welcomed freely and with honor by the abbot of each establishment.

Jaseen had relentlessly pushed us on toward these welcomed night stops each day, and to have one on this side of that mountain pass into Nepal had been an almost unbelievable miracle. Yet here it was. When we reached the wide gate in the high wall, Jaseen pulled the rope which dangled there in the wind. A bell clanged somewhere within, and almost immediately the gate swung open to reveal a red-robed monk, his shaven head like a bronzed dome over a very young-looking surprised face. With hardly a greeting, the monk bowed deeply and ushered us inside. We found ourselves in a spacious square courtyard paved with stone. A cold wind swept across its open forum, blowing the robes of three monks who ran toward us bowing and smiling, their faces clearly Mongolian Tibetan.

We followed one older monk into the temple, shadowy and mysterious now in the dusk, and we walked past the huge menacing god of the gate who guarded the temple hall, past the laughing Buddha. All the while, the wind blew in icily, fluttering the robes of the monks who came like bats out of the dimness to peer at us. They gathered around us as we came into the hall, for they wanted news of the outer world. They saw a foreign, white woman, and I sensed their awe as they stood speechless.

Somewhere inside the cavernous gompa, the immense hide drums sounded, followed by the deep-throated gongs, calling the monks to vespers. It was as strange as it was mysterious. The wind rushed through, stirring the red banners hanging from the rafters, and blew about the flames of the butter candles which always burned before the gods.

My mind closed against the murmur of voices, all speaking in Tibetan, asking hurried questions to Jaseen, who enjoyed his role with a flair of importance. There were stares at me, at Chanda, but Jaseen spoke carefully in his own shy polite manner. It was something I had learned with patience throughout this long, hard flight. Because I was silent, I knew my own esteem rose in the eyes of the monks.

In a few moments we were led to the small guest cells, always kept ready for pilgrims; Chanda and I shared one, and Jaseen was given another close by. A young monk hurried inside with a pewter lamp glowing warmly and set it down in the small room, then bowed himself out, leaving Chanda and me together. I glanced around the room, conscious of the thick stone wall, the thin hides stretched over the narrow window slits to keep out the icy drafts, and the thick heavy quilts folded for our use on the floor in one corner.

A deep fire pit was in the center of the room, and over the pit, high in the ceiling, was the inevitable hole for the smoke to be drawn upward; sometimes the wind brought a downdraft which could blacken the room with smoke.

At that moment, another monk entered, hurrying with glowing coals from another fire inside a deep iron pot. These he placed in the pit, pot and all, and placed dried yak dung on it. The coals caught and flames leaped up, and the monk bowed himself out of the door again.

It was all I could do to keep from falling down upon those quilts and allow my exhausted mind to float away, to shut out everything. But this was not to be, for Jaseen lifted the curtain and announced that we were to be guests of honor in the hall, at the abbot's invitation. "He say nurse not need come. Must stay here with child, eat here." He explained.

This suited Chanda well enough, as it did me. We should have time enough for a wash and to relax, however. Jaseen ducked out as another monk appeared bearing copper bowls of hot water for our wash; by this time, I realized it was the same smiling monk, grinning from ear to ear, always staring at me with those dark Mongolian eyes. I was perhaps the only Englishwoman ever to come to this corner of Nepal and his world.

He brought our tea and served it to us before he left us at last. It was the thick salted yak-butter tea which I had successfully acquired a taste for. I was grateful beyond my imagination for it at this moment, and I began to sip it contentedly, just as Chanda had started to do. It was restoring.

When I had finished, I set about to make use of the hot water, making sure the flaps on the door were tied down securely for privacy. I did not fancy having Peeping Toms, no matter how strange I might be to them.

I stripped down to my waist and began to scrub my face and neck and arms as best I could with the soap and cloth I pulled out from my pack. Chanda began to arrange the quilts on the low-built rope-thonged beds, and some of these she placed on the floor near the fire. Then she sat down cross-legged on one and calmly cradled Bianca's little son to her bosom, where he fed greedily on the milk she gave him. His contented little grunts were the only sounds in the room.

I glanced down at this woman who had lost her own baby even as Bianca's had lived, and every day of these past six months I had thanked my good fortune that Chanda had been willing to take care of this baby and follow me over the remote trails, running away from Khan Shayet's revenge, so that I could take this child to safety in Kathmandu. Had she not been available at that time, I shuddered to think what might have been his fate.

I began to brush the tangles from my long hair for a few free minutes before giving it a twist and repinning it in place on the back of my neck with four ivory hairpins. From the pack, I pulled out a clean camisole and hurried into it, then a fresh faded-yellow cotton shirt, full of sleeves and high rounded neckline, and tucked it into the heavy full homespun skirt I wore over two flannel petticoats, which were none too clean. Over this I pulled the long fur-lined soft suede tunic which served as my coat. I had time to pull on fresh cotton stockings, and then my boots, feeling somewhat the better for all the effort. Before I had finished replacing my articles in the pack, a voice from the door called out: "I bring food for Chanda. It's all right I come in?"

"Quite all right, Jaseen," I said, and stepped gingerly over the quilts to undo the flaps. I glanced back at Chanda. She had finished feeding the baby and placed him down beside her. Jaseen came inside carrying a pewter pot with a lid, and he put it down on the floor beside Chanda.

He stepped back, surveyed the room with a glance, then at me, with a very pleasant smile on his handsome young face. "Are you ready? It is time. I take you there."

I sighed, envying Chanda very much her ability to stay put, but I said, "Yes. I'm ready. Chanda? You get as much rest as you can. We shall leave here very early in the morning. Look" —I showed her the soap and towel—"I have left these out for you. Please put them back when you've had a go at them."

She spoke very little English, just those few words Bianca and I had managed to teach her, but she understood quickly, and along with the few words I knew in Urdu, Chinese and Turkistani, we managed well enough. Neither of us was prone to chatter anyway. Now, she said quite happily enough, "You go. Come back. Sleep." Her broad comfortable face smiled in the warmth of the room.

"That I hope to do," I said, trying not to sound cynical. "Now. Eat your dinner while it is hot." I turned again to Jaseen, who had gone back to the door. In the butter light his black hair glistened.

He was an unusually large young man. He wore a homespun shirt of faded-blue cotton under the woolen tunic, which covered the gray pantaloons that bloomed out over the soft leather boots which all nomadic country people wore; he carried a woolen shawl over his shoulder with dignity, and he was clean shaven. The woolly Russian hat he usually wore was now tucked inside a pocket under his arm. His skin was brown and smooth, and his liquid light-brown eyes had a sloe shape, which gave him his look of aloofness. Jaseen Gulag had a gentleness about him, but he had a proud isolation of his heart that I recognized as being like my own. A free spirit, not to be trapped or kept bound by unseen strings.

He had been unusually wily in outdistancing Khan Shayet; I could only guess at his pride in having brought us to this safety after weeks of dodging our enemy. He deserved as much respect and admiration as I could give him for this, but I did not say it. I was sure it would embarrass him.

"I'm ready now, Jaseen. We must say as little as possible of the truth as to why we are traveling down through this country. You understand, don't you?" I searched his eyes in the quiet moment, my voice low, even though we were still in the room.

"Have no fear. I tell why you must get to Kathmandu already."

I was surprised, but when he did not go on, I asked, "And what did you tell them?"

"No worry, please. I say bandit chief, very bad man, chase white English lady. I say Khan Shayet want white lady as his woman. Lady Harding wife of important English rajah in British residency in Kathmandu. Take baby son to husband. I take you to Lord Harding."

I burst out laughing. "Why, Jaseen! What a crafty mind you have! So I am a wife now, no less!" I laughed again.

"Not lie. Only just a little. Khan Shayet bargain for you in marketplace. Want English lady. I hear bad chief make boast. Not lie." He was adamant.

"So you told this to the priests here? That we escaped Khan Shayet by the skin of our teeth, because he was after me?" A shiver rushed over me, prickling my skin like fine needles of ice. "Very well. That is good enough, I suppose."

For a moment he was silent, just looking at me, and I knew he wanted to say something more.

"What is on your mind, Jaseen? Please say on."

"You not angry then? Make you Lady Harding only for safe journey. Married lady give better impression. Lord Harding, he won't know."

Annoyed, I hesitated. His conscience was bothering him, but mine wasn't. Lord Harding would just have to suffer it as I have suffered and for his cause, I had the thought. Oh, I was going to make him know it whenever I did meet up with him! But all this had nothing to do with Jaseen and his good intentions.

"Jaseen. You did the right thing. You are clever too, for thinking of it. It is much safer. Now. Let us go have that dinner. I'm famished, and I want to get back here as soon as possible." I glanced back at Chanda, who was watching us in her quiet manner. She nodded, and then Jaseen held up the curtain as we went out into the long corridor together. The wind tore at my skirts when we reached the doorless temple and we came into the guest hall.

Through the gaping doors of this great hall, I glimpsed the courtyard we'd come through earlier. It was darkened now with night, but inside the immense hall we stood in now, the pewter lamps burned in spite of the wind that swept through it unguarded, and the deep brazier pit in the center of the room was alive with burning coals.

Around it were placed dark-red cushions arranged for guests to sit upon, with small lacquered tables in front of each to use in dining. From where we stood, the hall looked grotesque, like a scene staged for ancient drama, incredibly unreal.

A monk from one of those doorless dark tunnels appeared with the wind flapping his robe and he bade me follow him; he guided me to my place, where the abbot of the monastery sat like a strange little gnome under his bright-yellow wind bonnet, buttoned under his chin, from which the long thin white beard fell over it like trails of cloud.

He sat in perfected meditation pose, cross-legged on three cushions stacked high so that it appeared as though he were sitting on a throne. But his eyes were bright and saw everything under their strange hooded lids.

The monk brought me to the right side of the Lamaist abbot, and returned to the shadows to bring Jaseen to his place to the left of the abbot, who would have the best advantage of both his guests.

Customary politeness forbade the abbot to hurry conversation until we were served tea, and at this point, six other monks filed in and took places around the glowing brazier, sitting cross-legged on the cushions as we sat, their backs straight in their red robes, the domes of their hairless heads gleaming like small bronze and brass gods in the flickering light.

A small boy-priest brought in beautiful little delicate jade bowls, and into each bowl he dropped tea leaves, then poured over them boiling water from a huge iron kettle. Wind tore at the steam from our bowls as we sipped it, silence still golden among us.

The bright eyes of our host missed nothing until our tea was being enjoyed; I knew I had never appreciated real tea as I did this bowl of tea; I knew too, that it was an unaccustomed luxury this night, served only because I was the abbot's guest.

The polite interchange of conversation began, with the abbot amazing me by speaking in excellent English; I was astonished further still when I learned that he had been as far east as Peiping, and as far west as London. He was concerned over my plight, an English lady being pursued by the notorious Khan Shayet.

He expressed his concern. "But you are indeed fortunate to have such a cunning guide to outwit this bad bandit chief, Lady Harding." I glanced at Jaseen, whose sheepish grin could not hide how he had exaggerated his tale. And although I thought I was prepared for it, I was shocked at being addressed as Lady Harding. The abbot's long beard, white as strands of silk, was blowing in the gush of wind against the dark-red robe as he talked on.

"You are safe now, Lady Harding. You need not fear that such a man as Khan Shayet will follow you across the gorge into our country. Only a prize higher than your person would entice Khan Shayet into the firing range of the Gurkhas. Such a man is full of avarice on all accounts. But he would bring himself to the attention of the royal maharaja's caravan too, which is now in the western interior of Nepal. I believe you may reach this party in time to travel on to the capital in their safekeeping."

"Thank you," I murmured, grateful indeed for this information. He spoke calmly with confidence, his wise old eyes never blinking as he studied me. Yet what he'd said brought a chill of uneasiness that touched me like a finger of ice. He was giving me a warning, and I knew it.

Only Khan Shayet himself knew what was in my possession and he wanted it, not my person. He would then stop at nothing to get it, and the old abbot sensed it, and he was probing. He saw more than I had wanted him to see.

"Do you know Khan Shayet then, Your Grace?" I asked, my voice husky with exhaustion as well as fear, even as the muffled notes of distant drums and the long sigh of the wind became not sounds but accents to the night around us.

"Who does not know of this much-feared man all along the highroads of China and Tibet and Kashmir? He is a chieftain of an Afghani Kirghiz tribe, a brigand who robs rich caravans, taking high prizes. He is to be respected, however, for his cunning mind is so full of guile, quite like a fox. 'Be careful of such a man' is the rule.

"Your being here, in his eyes, is a rare enigma, Lady Harding. What brought you to the highroads of the caravans at Leh in this time? We hear nothing but what the warring Zorawar Singh is doing there, of the devastation he has brought to overthrow the King of Ladakh. The dangers of an Englishwoman alone in such a strife-torn country is most peculiar. It places you in a situation that would attract attention." The old eyes scrutinized my face, and I was glad of the flame and shadowed room, for it hid much of my true feelings.

I allowed some brief minutes to pass before I spoke, and when I did, I told only the partial truth. "I was with my

brother, who had gone to Leh on official business." The old
man nodded, knowing of the attempted overthrow of the col-
lapsed dynasty in Leh by the invading Dogras from Jammu.
The intrigue in which my brother had played a most highly secret part as a spy for the British during the summer before. I
had thought at the time that it all had cost him his life, but
now I only said, "My brother had to leave quite suddenly, and
I was to follow, but that seemed impossible, and then the caravans came. I couldn't get through the Zoji La Pass, so I fled
with Jaseen and my son to Demchok. It seemed the only safe
route to Kathmandu. I hope to reach there as soon as possible."

The old abbot was interested, and he accepted this explana-
tion as if it pleased him, as though it were satisfactory, for he
did not mention it again. To my vast relief, several boy-priests
appeared with our supper.

Great bowls of steaming rice, and chunks of various vegetables with savory sauces and bean curd were placed before us;
there was no meat, as was to be expected in a Lamaist gompa,
but the fare was indeed a feast. Baked apricots and walnuts
were passed around, and afterward, the inevitable salted yak-
butter tea was poured into thin delicate bowls and passed to us.
I had been right in thinking that the green leaf tea had been a
luxury saved for honored guests.

It was all I could do to keep from snatching up the bowl of
rice before the abbot himself proceeded with a gesture of his
hand that the meal was opened and we should help ourselves.

As we ate, the abbot began to launch on a narrative of the
history of this monastery in the northwest corner of Nepal. It
was built by a wandering Buddhist monk from China who had
gone to Lhasa in Tibet, and had come in contact with the great
Tsong Khapa, the founder of the Yellow Hat Monks. He was
inspired studying under this great and revered priest.

It was from there that he decided to seek out a place in the
remote regions of the Gurla Mandhata Himalayas to give ref-
uge to pilgrims and to bring Buddha to the impoverished na-
tives in darkness. The abbot brought out an ancient manuscript

written in fine Tibetan print to show us the date of the build-
ing of the gompa in the year 1397.

It was an interesting story, but I found myself trying desperately to hold my eyes open. The abbot spared nothing in his
tale, and the other monks sat like stone gods, listening as if for
the first time. It all had the nightmare quality of some high ancient drama; even the drums had kept a steady pulsating beat
in the background with the wind, and I was caught up in it like
one who could not end the dream by waking.

When at last it was over and the abbot stood up to say a
polite good-night, I was amazed to see he was so short in stature. Yet he carried himself like a god, and he bowed graciously,
wishing me a good night's rest, and as I turned to leave the hall
I had the sensation that his eyes were following me even
through the windy shadows. I was sure he knew much more
than he let on about Khan Shayet. It made me uneasy, and I
brushed away sleep from my mind as Jaseen and I went back
along the corridor to our rooms.

At the door to my room, Jaseen whispered, as if he too, had
been affected by what the abbot had said, "Don't worry. I take
you to safety in the morning. We take yak and monk guide
down the mountain. One, two days maybe. Not to worry." His
eyes were large and luminous. "Bandit chief not follow."

He was reassuring me. "I'm sure you will get us there, Jaseen.
But we must rise early and be on our way. You were very brave
today. You saved our lives, risking your own to do it. Your
grandfather will be proud of you. We shall reach Kathmandu
because you will get us there. Thank you, Jaseen, and good
night. Get plenty of rest yourself." I smiled, though I felt
weary, and I saw his own smile. Then I slipped through the
curtain and tied the leather flaps firmly.

Chanda was already asleep, snoring gently, the baby pressed
close to her warm bosom. I noticed at once that she had pulled
out my fur robe from the pack and had arranged the quilts on
my bed near the still faint glow of the embers in the fire pit
across from where she slept.

I sank down on the quilts gratefully, removing my boots,

then placed more fuel on the embers in the pit. As the flames shot up, I undressed to my shift and pulled the fur robe around me as I lay down. The thin animal skins stretched across those narrow slits kept most of the draft out, but I knew there could easily be snow before morning in this high place, for it was the end of August.

Try as I might, sleep would not come, even though I snuggled down into the warmth of the fur. My mind was suddenly alive with all the fears and danger we still had ahead of us. I knew I could not rest easy until I was face to face with Lord Gordon Harding.

When I thought of this man who was directly responsible for my being in this ridiculous situation, all my rational thinking fled, leaving me consumed by the fury that had seethed inside me for the past year, fed by the insensitive manner in which he had used me!

It seemed a lifetime ago when I began this most incredible journey, and here I was on the rooftop of the world, crouched in fear for my very life, and running from a bloodthirsty brigand from the highroads of the silk and ivory and opium trade routes, fleeing with the little baby son of Lord Gordon's sister! When I did meet this man face to face, I vowed to spare him nothing in my wrath for all he had cost me in mental anguish as well as the physical discomforts I'd had to suffer throughout the whole year!

Lord Gordon Harding was a ruthless, hardhearted man. He had been responsible for the capture of my brother, Gavin Butler, by those so-called border police even while Gavin had been working as the undercover agent for him; meanwhile Lord Harding sat in the protective splendor of the incorruptible British facade cloaking his own dark diabolical deeds! Odious, horrendous creature! A—*Philistine*, I thought, trying to shut my mind to all the pent-up vile thoughts I had of this one man. But relief would not come so easily. I kept seeing all those people whom Lord Gordon had used to gain his own ends.

But then, the name of Harding had rankled darkly in the Butler family for centuries. Even before the great civil war, these two families had been enemies, the Hardings of Devon and the Butlers over into Cornwall. But during that war and in the Restoration afterward, it was outright bloodthirsty hate. The Hardings had been responsible for the Butlers' downfall, for their losing title and wealth, but more than this and closer to me, my own grandmother had suffered under the hands of the then Lord Howard Harding, Gordon's grandfather.

It was because of this that my grandfather, Sir James Butler, had taken to the adventurous life in the Far East, making runs across the Himalayas with those caravans and remaking the lost fortune of the Butlers. My own father, Sir William, had a more honorable way of life as an officer in Her Majesty's service and had lost his life in the disastrous retreat from Kabul, Afghanistan, three years before.

Yet it was Gavin who had come in contact with Lord Gordon Harding, and this man had used my brother ruthlessly. For all I knew, Gavin was dead and Lord Gordon had written him off without so much as a twinge of conscience, as serving above and beyond the call of duty. It made my blood boil.

My thoughts swerved back to Toby—Mr. Tobias Roberts. Faithful, strong and dependable Mr. Roberts! Was he also dead, his head severed from his body by the sharpened blade of a wicked scimitar swung by one of Khan Shayet's henchmen?

Toby had been with me through the thick of those treacherous weeks as we pursued Bianca and her captor, and when we had made the rescue in a blinding snowstorm, dear Toby disappeared after we escaped the Kirghiz camp. It was only in those last few days before he disappeared that I discovered just how much he meant to me.

Had Lord Gordon written Tobias Roberts off his list too? For Toby had been like a right arm to this man in all his private affairs, and he'd been unswerving in his loyalty above and beyond the call of duty. I wanted to cry, but all I could do was hate, and I could not stop my thoughts.

2

It was Mr. Roberts who had brought the letter from Lord Gordon to me in Srinagar, Kashmir, one year before. The shock of Gavin's strange disappearance had left me in a restless, unknowing state of mind, and I welcomed some form of action, although I would not have admitted that I wanted action from this source.

It had not come easy for me to know that I was twenty-seven, already a spinster with no great prospects of marriage, and with very little money of my own because an albatross in the form of a crumbling old manor house in Cornwall hung around my neck, with death duties eating away at the money Gavin and my father had provided.

Two years after our father's brave march out of the ill-fated city of Kabul and his subsequent death with his whole regiment, Gavin had insisted that I come out to Kashmir and keep house and company for him. I welcomed it with relief, and arrived in Srinagar just as winter was leaving and spring entered, barely a year after his invitation.

The lake was at its loveliest; it was the most exciting, momentous happening in my adult life, coming to Kashmir, the remote kingdom of lakes set in the Himalayas. It was one of the many places my grandfather had lived in and had left records of in the library of our Cornish home, Butlers Reach.

Gavin had leased a beautifully built house of rosy brick and timber set in an orchard overlooking Dal Lake near the Moghul gardens, and in it he had been extravagant beyond my imagination with the lovely carpets of silk and wool on the floors, and china imported from Peiping.

While Gavin was in Leh, the capital of Ladakh, on his missions, which I knew were secret, involving the political situation between Jammu and that country, with the British intervening, I kept house for my brother, and entertained. I was glad to get acquainted with my brother for the first time in our lives; he was three years older than I, and had left my life at a very early age. He was exciting, always living on the high keen tightrope of adventure as a top-secret agent for British intelligence; he was handsome too, and I suspected that he'd had his share of lovely ladies, but he'd never married.

When the news of his disappearance reached me, I knew no little fear, but as the weeks wore on, and I remained in the house above the lake, that fear faded. I had the family of Mohammud Gulag, who owned the house, and who had respected Gavin, to look after me.

I watched the high summer come in, knowing the days were idyllic and mine for an indefinite time, and I just let them ride by. The early rice was ready in the fields, and on the lower terraces of the mountains the farmers were cutting it, their sickles flashing in the midday sun like mirrors. Down on the lake, the willows fringed and shaded the canal and the waterways where the little kingfisher lived, and the lotuses were in flower, those great deep pink cups, resting on the giant flat green leaves, so thick and cool that they held pools of dew all day, glittering like diamonds at sunset.

In that setting, Mr. Roberts paid his unexpected call with the letter from Lord Gordon Harding in hand. After he had made himself known, we sat on the cool airy porch out of the hot sun, facing the lake below the village beyond my terraced gardens. Mohammud brought a jug of fresh lemonade, then left us.

With a glass of the cool drink in his hands, Mr. Roberts waited in unperturbed calmness, assured that everything was under control now that he was here. It was but for me to begin reading the letter he had given me.

I was disturbed even before I opened it, for those deep chords of distrust throbbed already inside me, ingrained in my whole being for the very name of this family. I could not quell that distrust as I opened the letter.

"My dear Miss Butler," the letter began sweepingly:

"On behalf of my sincere apologies, however belated they are, I am sending our man in Srinagar to hand this letter to you in person. It has just come to my attention that you have been living in Kashmir for quite some time; had I known of your presence out here, then I should have written to you before, as soon as it was apparent that your brother had disappeared somewhere along the highroads into China. Allow me to assure you, Miss Butler, that everything possible is being done to find your brother.

"I have regarded Gavin Butler as my friend as well as a close associate in all the affairs of our work out here. I place him high on my list as a brave and courageous man, worthy of the highest esteem.

"I recall your illustrious father, Sir William, and his services rendered to the Crown, above and beyond the call of duty, there in Kabul in January, 1842. None of us who are out here will forget that incident too soon. It did not escape my notice, and since Gavin was so closely connected, I can say he never once complained about his great loss there.

"It comes to me now that you must be feeling a double loss, and I want to reassure you again that we even now have a few bare traces of your brother which may indicate that he is not dead. Believe that."

I had glanced up from the letter after reading those first paragraphs, a sudden hope bursting within me, yet distrustful beyond reason. The words had reminded me of Gavin's laughing eyes and handsome bearded face all over again, and a strange new pain twisted around my heart. I met the eyes of "our man in Srinagar," in the form of Mr. Tobias Roberts.

He was probably near to Gavin's age and solid respectability lay upon him like a coating of dust, from the thick sandy hair and mustache, bushy above a firm determined mouth, to his fairly lean and impeccably clad form, in one of those khaki military suits so stiff without a crease which all Englishmen wear when they visit on official terms, and I realized at once that he did carry weight like that of a prince, faultlessly courteous, reliable, and with the capability to serve, no matter what crisis presented itself.

Even his eyes were a steady proper blue, and they met mine with all the propriety due to his station as well as mine. Yet I resented this. My feelings of loss about my father and my brother ran deep, and the fact that my family's known enemy, in spite of Gavin's connection with this man, was trying to reassure me that Gavin was not dead, seemed callous, and angered me beyond words.

On the other hand, I felt like bursting into tears, and it took all I could do in that moment to refrain from speaking out what I felt toward the man who had written the letter. Mr. Roberts, perhaps, would not understand that, so I bit my lips and lowered my eyes back to the letter, very disquieted.

"At this moment, Miss Butler," the letter went on, "a matter which is very urgent in my own private affairs has come to the surface, and I wish to engage your time and person while you are still bewildered, perhaps, in the uncertainty of Gavin's whereabouts. It may be that you would welcome something to take your mind off anxiety for your brother, to divert your grief to something outside yourself."

With something like a bitter echo, I recalled how Gavin had once told me of Lord Gordon's persuasive charm to use his staff members to gain his own selfish desires. I wanted to laugh, to mock this odious man and show him up for what he was. Yet, I read on:

"I have, unfortunately, a sister whose young age makes it imperative for me to look after her until she is safely married and in the keeping of a respectable and responsible husband. I regret to say she is a headstrong, self-willed young girl, quite immature for nineteen, and is very capable of ruining her life before it begins.

"She is, unfortunately again, the heiress to a vast fortune and estate, hers when she marries, or when she reaches twenty-five. I, being her only living relation and her brother, am the sole

protector of her interests, and I find it more of a baffling prob-
lem to subdue her miscreant spirit as time wears on. Her wild
escapades are indeed causing undue embarrassment to everyone
responsible for her welfare.

"She has a temperament which makes it impossible for me
to help her, I must admit, partly because of my work here in
Nepal, which keeps me from taking her into my custody when
she so needs it. My sister has given much grief to those in my
employment to care for her, various governesses of the past and
companions all her young life. I spared nothing as far as she is
concerned, to her interests, so that you will know what you are
up against. She has run away from the latest school in London
which I had arranged for her to attend, somehow eluding the
headmistress with the cunning mind of a little vixen. In short,
Miss Butler, she is a little hellion that I would like to see
tamed, and she needs a firm hand by someone with no nonsense.

"In my belief, you are that person, Miss Butler. Gavin mentioned you more than once in our many conversations. He always admired you for being level-headed, as he put it, with no
nonsense whenever you had to cope with the most trying of sit-
uations with your past students, and always discreet in making
decisions. I have a most excellent report of your sterling character. That, and the fact that we, our families, that is, have been
neighbors for centuries, in our homeland, doubles my belief
that you are the right person to take my sister in hand. Allow
our ancestors' past grievances to lie buried with that past, Miss
Butler, I pray you."

An outrageous gasp escaped me as I continued to read that
letter, every word scorching across my brain, while I was astonished beyond belief. Gavin? How could my brother have
recommended me? He had not known of the scandal I had
been involved in eight years ago, so he wouldn't have known
the great crisis which had brought our father back to Somerset
from his duty in India. No. Gavin would never have been able
to give an excellent report of my sterling character!

Mr. Roberts was quietly observing my face, and it dis-

comfited me; but the absurdity of this letter aroused my ire:
the man was impossible, with his belief that he could, with the
turn of a quill on paper, engage anyone to do his own distasteful duty!

I couldn't have spoken had I wanted to at that moment, so I
read on.

"I have been informed that Bianca left her godmother's
house in a most deceitful manner, boarded a ship which no one
seemed to be able to trace, but apparently bound for Persia, in-
tending to rendezvous somewhere on the top of the world with
one notorious soldier of fortune, an Englishman making illicit
and illegal runs by caravan between China and Afghanistan. I
can learn nothing as yet of his origin, except that he is young,
bold, and aggressive, and imagines himself to be an adventurer.

"I believe he comes from a poor but genteel family, but
spends his time preying on young defenseless heiresses, my
sister his latest victim. How she ever came in contact with this
scoundrel, I cannot conceive, but heaven help him when I do
set my hands on his throat!

"My scouts have informed me that David Markus is crafty
and unreliable where his word is concerned. I fear greatly for
my sister, who would throw herself on his mercy and receive
none when she might need it.

"She is now en route to Srinagar, I have been informed by
reliable sources. I want her to be intercepted there, for it could
be the last stand in a civilized hill station before she encounters
Markus. He dares not show his face there, I am certain. If he
does, then he is a fool. But I believe he is too crafty to try anything so openhanded.

"Bianca, I must warn you, Miss Butler, is also capable of any
trick in the book, and she will try to deceive you from the beginning. Mr. Tobias Roberts can give you in full detail what
you may want to know, and just where my sister is most likely
to take lodgings once she arrives there. No effort will be spared
to help you intercept her, yet it all must be kept subtle, so that
she won't renege and spoil your efforts to win her over to see
sensibility as well as discretion.

"I implore you to consider my offer. Stop her at all cost from meeting up with David Markus. I have given Tobias authority to hand you a draft for an unlimited amount of money that you may need for expenses. Use it liberally. Tobias is to hand you a bonus in advance also, for your services to me."

I was stunned at the amount he mentioned; it quite took my breath, knocking the winds from my set sail to refuse him; my hands shook as I read on before dropping the letter into my lap.

"I shall be indebted to you, should you be able to bring about what others have not done, Miss Butler. Bring her to Nepal, for I believe the local color in the royal court is full enough of intrigue to capture her attention for the moment. The British residency is adequately comfortable, and she would be under my care, even pressured if necessary for the next five years. I should want you to remain with her as a constant companion, and I trust you to use your good judgment and common sense during that time.

"Tobias will arrange all travel and accommodation for you, and he will aid you in any situation that arises concerning my sister. I trust him implicitly, and so may you.

"May I say again that you may be reassured that everything possible is being done to locate your brother. I wish you the best in this venture ahead of you. Remember, she has a wily nature, so be forewarned. In all regards, I am sincerely in your debt."

It was signed: Lord Gordon Harding.

*

The events from that day to this hour, where I lay huddled under the fur robe in the ancient Lamaist gompa guest room, had gone far beyond the wildest imagination that I could ever have perceived when I'd first read that letter.

Nothing in my previous experience in life had prepared me for what was to follow, even when I looked up from reading it, angry as I was and quite indignant that Lord Gordon could even assume that I would accept his offer, and met the steady blue gaze of Mr. Tobias Roberts.

He'd been studying me and my appearance from the moment he'd sat down, and I had the cool little thought that he had already summed up the situation. I had no idea what he knew of my brother, if he had known him, in fact, or what he knew about our families, of our lost heritage in the Restoration period, and of the bitter humiliation with which the Hardings had visited upon the Butlers.

He spoke first. "Miss Butler. You have no idea just how important this request from Lord Gordon is. I hope you will not hesitate to accept his generous offer, and I can certainly reassure you that you won't regret it. I have the draft already drawn up in your name." He brought out a packet from his briefcase, and handed it over to me. I took it, without even opening it, making an effort not to spurt out a hasty refusal.

"You know then, the contents of this letter?" Of course he did, I thought, somehow annoyed by everything: the way his polite steady blue eyes searched my face annoyed me, as did the warm sandy hair springing up from his high forehead, and the waiting patience he bore like a shield.

He nodded to my question. "Yes. The contents have been disclosed to me. I might say, in regard to Lord Gordon's offer, that it is most generous of him, for not in all of my knowledge of his engaging any other young woman for his sister's care has he been more generous than now. But then, you have been well recommended, Miss Butler. I have no doubt that was the reason Lord Gordon could entrust his sister to your care."

I bristled like a hedgehog. "My brother's praises, Mr. Roberts? How could he recommend me, and to something he could not even foresee?" I was at once suspicious.

He was unperturbed. "That is true, quite true, I daresay. It was a Lady Pearson who vouched for your sterling character, and it was a most glowing report of praise, I understand. You have every reason to believe Lord Gordon's trust in your abilities."

"Lady—Pearson?" I was stunned, staring at the man in dis-

belief. That name brought slivers of old fears slicing through
my heart. How could she have recommended me to anything
but pain? And why, after all those years, should she and Sir
Lyle change their minds? Lady Gillian Pearson had been ada-
mantly unforgiving in those weeks following the tragedy, and
when my father had asked them to remember my youth and
not hold what had happened to me and to them a grudge for
the rest of our lives.

I could almost hear Lady Gillian's cold voice even now as
she had said: "I cannot and I won't forgive your daughter for
the treachery and deceit she has clearly revealed in her character, Sir William. Youth? Bah! Impulsive, impetuously wanton
creature! Tawny Butler will have to learn a much harder lesson
in life as she goes from my home, where she had been received
and given privileges as we would have given them to our own
daughter. I will not forgive her."

Eight years ago. How did it happen that Lord Gordon Harding could have a letter from them? And why should she have
changed her mind? I simply could not believe this to be true.

"Indeed, Mr. Roberts?" I heard my voice take possession and
say coldly, "I am sure Lady . . . Pearson could have little, if
any, reason to recommend me to this post. How could she have
come to Lord Gordon's attention in this matter?"

If all the bitterness and heartache I felt inside me was clearly
revealed in that one sentence, Mr. Roberts gave no indication
that he saw it.

"I say, Miss Butler, I have no way of knowing the answer to
that. Their families have been on friendly terms for several
years now, I understand." He cleared his throat and then
changed the subject, as if it didn't matter one whit whether or
not Lady Pearson had changed her mind.

"Lord Gordon's sister is somewhat of an impetuous young
woman, a child still, who needs a firm but gentle touch to help
her in this most difficult period, in my own opinion. She lost
both of her parents at an early age, and such instructions as
only a mother could give to a talented young girl were denied
her completely, it seems."

His words were fitly chosen; they subdued the ire I was seeth-ing with, and after a moment, I said with less cynicism, but guardedly, "You know Miss . . . Harding then?"

"Her ladyship is known to me, I daresay."

"So she carries a title, then. Lady—?" I stopped.

"Lady Bianca Harding," he finished for me.

"Of course," I said, recalling her name mentioned in the let-ter. "I see. And why doesn't Lord Gordon have his men inter-cept her, and carry her forcibly to Nepal, as I seem to get the impression he would like to keep her under lock and key until she comes of age?" I bristled, feeling the surge of resentment as well as contempt rising like gall to my lips. "If he knows where she is in Asia, I hardly see what point engaging me would have, when he can simply take her by force."

This had no effect on his confidence at all. "That would not do at all, Miss Butler. Lord Gordon knows that with the slightest opposition his sister would resist and cause a scandal which could have major results in certain diplomatic relations. You do understand, do you not, Miss Butler, that from the viewpoint of protocol, every step must be carefully weighed and not one shred of scandal touch Lord Gordon's name while he is in Nepal at this time? He is counting on protocol. She must come, with your persuasion, of course, of her own accord. To act rashly would serve no purpose."

"Of course I understand," I said with a trace of mockery in my voice, while every nerve inside me screamed out to attack, but this was the wrong man to attack. "Perfectly so. Surely, though, I cannot be expected to do what others have failed so far to do. If she is so cunning, as her brother writes of her, as to have outwitted all the others he has placed in charge of her," I said, noting the audacity of it all, "she can also outwit me. I fail to see just where I can change a rebellious teen-ager, which she has obviously proven herself to be, into a mature adult, or into a meek young girl, which Lord Gordon seems to want done during this *charade.*"

How steady and direct his eyes were, with all the confidence he had in his employer! It almost unnerved me, for he did not resent my sarcasm, or even laugh it to scorn.

"Lord Gordon is fully aware of the possible setbacks, to be sure, Miss Butler. I believe he merely wants to happen what is in her best of interests. We can only assume that if you accept his offer, she just may respond. You see, I am of the firm opinion that Lady Bianca wants to go to stay with her brother. I believe she has wanted to have his full and undivided attention. I think she has tried, unsuccessfully, to get his attention, and has resorted to a sort of blackmail to get it. Now, this is all my own private opinion, as a bystander, looking on."

"I see," I said slowly, thinking that this was highly unusual, but rather interesting. "Have you spoken of this to Lord Gordon?"

"It is not something we have discussed, no. I will admit, however, that he is sincere in his duty toward her, and that he has complete faith in your ability to persuade her to change her mind about meeting this David Markus."

"Based solely upon the recommendation of Lady Pearson? He seems to have this unusual faith in someone he knows very little of." How scornful my own words sounded. He smiled; it was a sunny smile, very warm and unaffected, making my barbed words distasteful as well as unkind, even to me. It struck me then that Mr. Tobias Roberts was as solid and steady as a rock, never swerving in his loyalty, and just as pleasant.

"That, my dear Miss Butler, I have no way of knowing, although it was a splendid one. And meeting you verifies it all."

At once I was ashamed of my scornful wrath, so witlessly spoken. For a moment I could not speak, and so I glanced down to the unopened packet in my lap. Impulsively I opened it, thinking that not for all the tea in China or for Lady Gillian Pearson's recommendation and forgiveness did I want to be saddled with a runaway spoiled heiress. I'd had enough of them during these past four years to last a lifetime.

Thus, as I pulled the money from the packet, I had a sense of overwhelming defeat. The sum of it stunned me, for it was a stupendous amount, more than I could earn in a lifetime teaching young heiresses the proper graces of being ladies. I glanced up, bewildered. "There must be some mistake—"

He shook his head. "There is no mistake, I can assure you, Miss Butler. Lord Gordon is rather keen on your accepting his offer. Nothing less would have been adequate, to his way of thinking." His voice was a little gruff, but not unkind.

"So it appears," I said, annoyed with myself for no reason at all. I sat in an uncomfortable moment of silence, my eyes catching the flight of the bulbul from the edge of the almond tree to perch on the porch banister, golden with his plumage shimmering in the light. Then I looked at Mr. Roberts. "It could prove too great a task for one woman to achieve. And should I accept the offer," I said slowly with meaning, "and fail to guide Lady Bianca into the maturity her brother so desires for her, what then, Mr. Roberts?" I glanced down at the money in my hands, then back at him. "A girl already nineteen, with a self-will to deceive the very best of adults, can hardly turn meek and allow a perfect stranger to take the reins of her future in hand."

I was probing. To turn this offer down now, would be throwing away a rare challenge, I knew, and I wanted everything to be clear. I knew it was the money which enhanced my sudden change of mind, but there had to be an understanding.

"That is taken into consideration. We cannot help what fails beyond our power. But the money is yours, whatever the outcome. You can be well assured that Lord Gordon fully understands just what risks there are involved, and where he is placing you, when it comes to his sister. You have but to accept the offer, and this other draft"—he brought out another packet from the briefcase and handed it to me—"is yours also. Expenses can be tiresome, but I'm sure you will find all this ample to cover them." He smiled indulgently, the light in his eyes warm behind the blue.

He knew then, as well as I did, that I had mentally accepted this highly unusual offer. One spoiled heiress might just as well be my lot now as the prospect of going back to England and picking up where I'd left off with several snobbish girls of the upper class.

"Am I right in saying that I should write an agreement to Lord Gordon to accept his offer, then?" I folded the letter and with the money, replaced it in the packet, knowing it was settled in my mind.

He inclined his head to one side, and leaned back in the cane chair. "I will write him, Miss Butler, to say you've done so. I think it doesn't need to be said that if you accept the draft and the money as a bonus for your efforts, that you have accepted the post. It is sealed, then, and with your signature on this document, we shall conclude the matter, and I will send it to Lord Gordon." He handed me a written document, which after scanning briefly I signed my name with the quill pen he had ready for me.

While he dusted the ink with drying powder, and began to replace it in his case, I poured more lemonade into his glass. He accepted it graciously. And then, I asked: "Have you any knowledge of just where Lady Bianca may be at this moment?"

"Yes. I do in fact know that she is lodged here in Srinagar, on the far side of Dal Lake, in a most disreputable wayside inn for caravans passing through Kashmir." He frowned thoughtfully.

I could not hide my astonishment. "So she is here, then." I breathed, and I knew I had anticipated at least some time before I should meet her, perhaps to get myself used to the idea.

"She arrived yesterday, in an elephant caravan from Rawalpindi."

"But this is most astounding, Mr. Roberts!" I declared. "If you know where she is, then you must know what her intentions are. . . ." I stopped, uneasily puzzled that he should be so calm about it. "Does she know about you? And—forgive me if I seem bewildered—but can she know of her brother's intentions?"

"Yes, indeed. I went to her the first thing this morning before coming out here to you. She is well informed of what Lord Gordon has in mind."

I was more amazed than before. "Did she—object?"

He shook his head, taking a long swallow of the fruit drink, then set the glass down on the tray on the table between us. "Not Lady Bianca. It was she who contacted me at the residency, informing me of her arrival last evening, sending a note over early this morning. She didn't object in the least when I gave her brother's letter to her, but rather, she seemed to accept it all in a resignedly good grace. Which led me to conclude that she just may want her brother's care. It's most reassuring, don't you think?"

I didn't answer that, for I couldn't; it seemed to all go against what Lord Gordon had written of his sister. But I asked, "Then I take it she has not yet kept her rendezvous with the young man in question?"

"No. He seems to have stood her up, and she is a little dazed by it all, I believe. I should think it our gain if we take our action now, Miss Butler, and move in on her at once. I want to introduce you to her, and as soon as possible, while she is apparently having second thoughts about that wild escapade she could have with David Markus."

"Hmn-mn. I see what you mean. Yes. Should we go at once, then?"

"It would be advisable. Are you prepared to accompany me now?"

"I should think it my duty, Mr. Roberts," I said.

"Very well, then. But I implore you to try to persuade her to leave the inn, and today, if it can be done. It is a most unsavory place, and I distrust that landlord! If I may suggest it, perhaps it would be to your advantage to invite Lady Bianca to stay here with you, until such time as we can arrange travel to Nepal, more favorable when the monsoon is over in September." He didn't blink an eyelash. I saw his meaning.

"So that she won't have a chance to meet this David Markus, should he just happen to materialize and persuade her to go with him?" I couldn't resist saying.

"Quite right, Miss Butler. We understand each other." He smiled back at me.

"Yes. Then I do agree it should be well for her to come here with me. It will be to her advantage as well as mine." I stood up. "Then, if you will permit me a quarter of an hour, I shall accompany you. I will want to inform my houseboy, so that they too, will expect us."

"Very good, Miss Butler." And he stood beside me, a man of average height, with broad shoulders. "I knew you would see it like that."

I left him then, and walked into the house; the parlor and dining room were already in the quiet yellow shade of the canvas awnings stretched out like giant butterfly wings from the windows. Gavin had brought the awnings up from Bombay when he'd come to meet my ship in early March. The yellow left a soft light to the beautifully polished wood paneling, and I moved up the carved wooden staircase to my rooms on the upper floor, knowing my mind had suddenly begun to stretch and deepen with this new challenge.

It even occurred to me that my life prior to that moment had gone quite stale and sour, and yes, empty after Gavin's disappearance. This then, could easily be the challenge I needed. A little thought shot up in my mind that Lady Bianca just might be difficult, and that our personalities would clash, but I pushed that aside to cross that bridge when I came to it. I had no qualms, and wanted none, about giving myself over to a challenge I needed.

Perhaps it was due to the enigma of Lady Gillian Pearson's sudden forgiveness after all these years; yet I did not want to dwell on those thoughts, and I successfully brushed them aside and gave myself to what lay ahead of me in this day.

The limp cotton morning gown I wore clung to my damp skin, and I stripped it off and carefully sponged my hot skin with cool violet water, then removed the pins which held my hair in its heavy knot, and began to brush the long honey-colored strands. This cooled my head considerably. I then rearranged my hair into a smooth curve around my face and fastened the knot on the nape of my neck with the ivory pins.

I didn't hesitate as to what I should wear, but pulled out my coolest and lightest gown: the pale-amber muslin with the wide skirt and lace inserts, with lace around the low décolleté neckline and at the elbows. It fell over my petticoats and the crinoline like watered silk, and when I glanced in the mirror I was amazed to see that my eyes had a strange new light behind them, and my color was high. Oh, yes, I felt I was somehow a different creature already.

With a careful glance in that same mirror, I composed myself and slowly pulled on the lace mitts; I placed the money and the letter in the reticule which was attached to my skirts, and then picked up the lace-trimmed parasol. I was ready; hardly had that quarter of an hour passed when I descended the stairs and returned to the porch, where Mr. Roberts was talking with old Mohammud Gulag, Jaseen's grandfather, the man who owned my house.

Mohammud's family worked the land, tended the gardens, and made carpets down in their house on the lake. Mohammud himself was my cook, and Jaseen was the houseboy. Jaseen's father was a guide for the English who went in and out of Ladakh. The family had liked Gavin and my loss was their loss, Mohammud had told me.

They turned as I joined them, and I said, "Mohammud, I am going out with Mr. Roberts now. But I shall return, possibly with a young lady to stay as my guest for some time. Perhaps you will get Jaseen to clear my brother's room and ready it for her. Fresh linens and flowers, I think." I smiled at the old man. He was as brown as a walnut, and didn't look his grand age of nearly eighty—not in the least.

"I will see to it. And dinner?" He glanced knowingly at Mr. Roberts.

Mr. Roberts took his cue before I could say anything. "I shan't be joining the ladies for dinner, Mohammud." He looked at me knowingly, but Mohammud merely bowed his head, touching his forehead with his finger in a gesture that he understood, and waited politely.

"If I can persuade Lady Bianca to come back with me this day, then it shall be dinner for two, Mohammud."

"Very well," he said, and I thought I saw speculation in the old but strangely light eyes in that ancient face with its patriarchal beard and the Moslem wrapped turban he wore with dignity. But again, he only touched his forehead in that gesture that said he understood, and watched Mr. Roberts and me walk down the garden path to the gate where the carriage and driver waited.

He was still watching us as we drove off between the tall, almost golden poplar trees down to the road that skirted the lake.

3

Dal Lake was a pearl of water and flowers set between the mountains, and was fringed by lacy weeping willow trees. The mountains stood out clearly, blue and dry with purple shadows, and down on the lake they reflected on the water, breaking the intense blue of reflected sky as well.

When I had arrived in late winter, the pink from the almond groves, the yellow of the first crocus and mustard, the pale crystal blue of the sky, the white cherry blossoms and clouds, and the green from new willows down along the waterways and canals created visions of poetry and romance.

Even as I traveled over the ancient caravan route, which the Moghul emperor Jahangir had used when he first entered the Vale of Kashmir from Delhi, I had been enchanted. From the lowest terrace, where cherry and almond trees were white and pink against the green of the mountains, the view was breathtaking. Downward, almond and cherry blossoms were pink and white against the blue water of the lakes.

For the Vale of Kashmir was a chain of lakes and rivers, set with orchards and gardens in a ring of snow mountains. The water came down off the glaciers on those far Himalayan peaks, cascading down through the passes until it fell to the Vale floor and flowed into its lakes and rivers.

Those colors had deepened and grown rich with late spring and summer; other greens from the old chenar trees in the Moghul gardens of Shalimar and Nishat, from the velvet grass, the rice on the narrow steps terraced up the mountains, and the purple from lilacs and vivid splashes of scarlet tulips. I felt I had been a witness, a part of it, as I watched it change.

And now it was high summer. We skirted the lake, heading
for Dal Gate, where the River Jhelum flowed into the lake.
From the beginning, Kashmir had been a part of India.
Buddhist and Hindu had thrived side by side for centuries, and
many temples and shrines of both religions had been built.
During the sixteenth century, however, Kashmir was invaded
and conquered by the Moghuls, who were Moslems.

The Moghul fort, rising on Hari Parbath Hill, its walls always red in sunrise and sunset, dominated Srinagar with Dal
and Nagin lakes at its base, and a beautiful mosque had been
built beside the ancient Hindu temple.

When the Moghul empire crumbled in the last century
under the pressure of the maharajas of Jammu and more re-
cently, with the British intervention, Kashmir came under the
rule of a Hindu maharaja at the new treaty of Amritsar.

During our ride into Srinagar, we were mostly quiet, each in
our own thoughts. It occurred to me more than once that Mr.
Roberts must have known my brother, yet I was reluctant to
speak of Gavin, and he didn't volunteer. But he did tell me
that he came to Srinagar as often as he could.·

"Mostly, my job takes me to Calcutta or Delhi. It is a relief
to get away from those places and come to a paradise like Kashmir. Have you been down on the lake, in the backwater, Miss
Butler? Those houseboats being built there as summer resi-
dences are very unique, and I say, I fancy one of them myself."

I assured him I had taken a shikara through the canals to
Nagin Lake; mostly, this was mere polite chatter and we
crossed the bridge to follow the Jhelum River, which wound
like a serpent through the old city.

Life throbbed with all its joys and sorrows on this river; flat
vegetable boats came in from the strange floating gardens out
of the backwater of Nagin Lake, laden with huge melons, to-
matoes, cucumbers and fresh greens to be sold every morning
to merchants and to anyone shopping for the ripe summer
fruits. The flower boats came too, laden to the gunwales with
every variety of fresh flower, making violet and pink and scarlet
and green reflections in long colorful panels on the water. Shi-

karas, the canopied boats which passengers relaxed in, glided gracefully down the river bearing prosperous merchants to their homes or businesses on the lake.

Houseboats lined the river where whole families lived together. It always came as a shock when I came face to face with the poverty along the riverfront after having been in the fruitful villages above the lake, with the rich fields of plenty where the farmers worked in the sun, their women pounding the ripe grain and then grinding it in the hand mills beside the canals. I had watched them spin their wool and flax, while their men smoked contentedly on their water pipes, those strange hookahs that bubbled soothingly as they sucked upon it. Life in the rich countryside could turn me into a romantic poet, but the squalor I saw today hit me as it always did: life and death were companions here along the river frontage, which we followed until we came to the Hari Parbath Inn.

It took a while to get through the city, for it was just after midday. The streets were crowded, and the driver had to use his skill to push the horse between the shops in the narrow crooked lanes, but at last we approached the thick stone Moghul Bridge that arched over the Mar Canal.

The inn was located at this junction, in the curve, sprawling with its back right on the canal. It was an ancient structure of faded-red brick and wooden balconied rooms that perilously overhung the back waterfront, where most of the business transpired. Its front spilled out into a huge walled-in courtyard adjacent to the narrow dusty street that was a hubbub of movement and change.

Our driver swung the carriage into the courtyard; around us swirled the enigmatic caravans from the whole heartland of Asia. I felt a thrill of excitement stir up all that sense of wild adventure and romance, seeing the caravans coming and going.

Men that had crossed and recrossed the high routes over the Oxus and the Indus rivers, coming from more than a thousand miles away, found their way here. Tall men from tribes in old kingdoms I did not know existed, with their tanned beautiful faces and smiles, dressed in fur boots and leather tunics, driving camels from Mongolia, and yaks, horses and pack mules, were here. There were elephants and the white-turbaned Sikhs who drove them over the Banihal Pass to Jammu and Rawalpindi; caravans going and coming from India and Afghanistan to Sinkiang, Kashgar, Turkistan and Yarkand, to Leh through the Zoji La Pass. North, south, east, west; all caravans swung crazily into this courtyard.

It occurred to me that Lady Bianca had chosen this place to lodge in because of a free and uninhibited spirit; it was the one thing that often cried out inside my own turbulent but curbed spirit. I wanted to be set free and to follow with abandon all the desires and dreams in search of myself! It made me think of my grandfather and of Gavin, who had followed these routes like a migrating bird. Did this young untamed heiress, whose impulsive nature I was sent to curb, feel this strange exciting movement? I could almost envy her, and in some ways I did, even without having met her.

These were my thoughts as Mr. Roberts helped me down from the carriage to stand beside him at the yawning entrance of the inn.

"She couldn't have chosen a more ideal inn to lodge herself in if she intended to keep her rendezvous with Mr. Markus," I said, more to myself than to him. And I silently wondered if this David Markus had, indeed, arranged it for her in advance.

Tobias Roberts seemed suddenly affronted; his voice was gruff when he said, "She should have gone to the residency. Nedou's is the logical place for a young unprotected lady. I'm surprised that she even considered staying here. Markus is a scoundrel if he arranged this, and he could have very little respect for her person to even suggest it! I don't like the looks of this. Cutthroats, every last one of them. Oh, I say, Miss Butler. You must do your best in persuading her to leave this place."

He looked at me; the sunlit dust swirled like a bright fog around us, and his eyes narrowed with that light in them. I saw that he was annoyed and by everything. The unpleasant odorous sweaty bodies, the strong smells of leather, hay and dung clung close to the very air in the heat of noon. It irritated

him like sand rubbed on raw skin, I thought, and I don't know
why I felt as detached from it as I did in that moment. Nothing was offensive to me, as it seemed to be for him.

Before I could reassure him that I would do my best to lure
Lady Bianca away as he wished me to do, a voice called out
behind us, and we turned, startled. It was the girl herself,
dressed in a long white burnoose cut so simply that it made her
look regal in spite of her diminutive form.

"Dearest Toby! What suspense you have kept me in! I
thought you'd never arrive, and I'm famished. I've just this
hour ordered our lunch, and thank heavens you've come. It's
most crowded in here, but we do have a small room I've engaged for our meal, and we can talk in relative quiet there."

I had one profound and lasting impression of this young
woman whom I'd been hired to guide into maturity: she could
never be the little hellion her brother had so erroneously
branded her. The hood which covered her hair fell back a little
as she looked up at Tobias Roberts, who towered like a giant
over her, and revealed bright penny-copper curls, framing a
heart-shaped face that was young and poignantly expectant,
and there was not a trace of that guile which Lord Gordon had
almost convinced me I should discern.

Tobias Roberts seemed a gruff fatherly figure scowling down
at her. "Lady Bianca," he said, but not unkindly, "I had
thought to take you from this place and have our dinner at
Nedou's Hotel. We'd be far more comfortable there."

She blinked her wide eyes, and I noticed how very candid
they were. "That is so like you to be so thoughtful, dear Toby.
But I should not want to offend the proprietor here—not now,
after putting him to so much trouble seeing to the room we're
to have. He was ever so kind, and with all the demands made
upon him with all these people coming and going, he even had
the room scrubbed and cleaned so that we should be comfortable during our meal. You must agree to this, and we shall then
retire this very minute to the room, after you have introduced
me to Miss Butler."

She became almost shy then, as her eyes left Tobias and

touched mine. There was nothing else he could do, after so pretty a speech, and he became all protocol as he introduced us. "I say, but I do hope you'll be friends."

"And why ever should we not be friends, Miss Butler?" She held out her hand and as I took it in a firm handshake, I noticed the light warm tan of her skin as the sleeve fell back.

"I see no reason at all, Lady Bianca," I said, smiling down into those great pansy-like eyes. I saw too, a fine sprinkling of light freckles across the pert nose. I was anxious that this first meeting should be on a sound basis of trust, and I was certain that she must have been thinking along the same lines as we stood there in that brief moment. She looked like a little girl, for she was much shorter than my own tall person.

"There." She smiled, a tiny dimple playing at the far corner of her full pink mouth, almost innocently provocative. "So it is settled. We shall get along famously. Now," she turned, "our host, Samsar Chand Koul, is waiting for us. See how he smiles? He is ever so anxious to please." We followed her into the thriving den of the not too clean inn.

Tobias said darkly, "My word, Lady Bianca. I dare say that with you as his paying guest, he can hardly have a better reason to please." He glared ominously at the man who came toward us.

"Welcome to Hari Parbath Inn," he said, nearly bowing himself to the floor. His long thin face was bean-brown and he had a voice of honey and oil, and I distrusted him as I knew Tobias Roberts did. He wore a dirty gray pheran, the loose robe which all Kashmiri men wore, and because he was a Moslem, he wore a white turban of folded muslin.

Mr. Roberts took complete charge of the situation, expecting immediate attention, which won him instant respect. The man nearly snapped to his command. "Take the ladies to the room, and make sure no one follows them. I shall inform my driver that we shall be staying." He turned to us. "I shan't be but a moment. Then I will join you." To the bowing proprietor, he said sternly, "Carry on."

"Very good," Samsar Chand Koul said, touching his forehead quickly to Tobias. He turned then and led the way across the noisy crowded room of foreign nationals who mingled here. We knew that the strange dark eyes of the caravan drivers were upon us, two Englishwomen.

The room was a curious low-ceilinged affair, smoky and dark with centuries of use, the heavy beams blackened with age. The smell of leather and unwashed bodies was strong, along with the scents from food cooking in the open kitchens that faced the water canal front. Voices in the quick alien tongues were raucous and ebullient, with the hauntingly sad strains that came from the old street musician rising above it all in snatches from the open windows.

When the man in front of us opened the door, we were ushered into a room that surprised me with its airiness in spite of the smallness. It opened onto a balcony; I caught glimpses of green sunny willows and the canal and scarlet flowers and kingfishers darting like blue and orange blazes across my vision.

An attractive table of polished walnut was in the center of the room, with a low round bowl of pink and yellow roses arranged so that their petals reflected in the shining surface. The chairs looked comfortable, and there was a comfortable sofa in deep-red mohair near the open balcony doors. We should all be quite easy together in here, I thought, noting also the three places set at the table. But then I wondered why uneasiness crowded in on the skirts of my mind as the afternoon wore on, when all seemed to be going so well.

The landlord bowed, smiled and turned to Bianca. He had been charmed by this correct little English lady, perhaps to the point of being overconfident that she just might fall into his greedy hands in her unprotected state. But now she informed him politely that as soon as Mr. Roberts returned, he could start serving the meal. She dismissed him with such a regal manner that even I was astonished.

That I had expected a temperamental, selfishly inclined rich girl was obvious in my astonishment. She was soft-spoken, rational and, above all, completely unmatched in her perfected, proper manners.

"Yes, my lady," the man said, bowing, his eyes going to my face as if he were trying to make up his mind just where I fit in with this apparently wealthy young woman. Then he touched his forehead with two fingers and backed from the room, closing the door behind him.

She turned to me, relieved. "Miss Butler . . . Tawny. What a strange unusual name! But, it matches you, you know. You have that color. I wonder if your mother looked at you and thought of those colors when she named you?" She surprised me by speaking so dreamily and being so outspoken with her thoughts.

"My mother died when I was very young, so I can't know just what she did think. In any case, I believe it may have been my father who influenced her in the choice of my name," I said lightly.

She studied me for a brief second. "They're nearly yellow; no, not yellow, I think. A cloudy, greenish amber. For eyes, that's most disturbing and unusual."

She made me uncomfortable with her keen observance. "Most people would say they are cat's eyes," I said, laughing, trying to hide my uneasiness. "You are very romantic and poetic, Lady Bianca." But I was not displeased that she had noticed.

Her eyes widened, and I saw that they were almost celestial blue in their color. "Oh. But you must have been hurt by someone who said that about your eyes—as a child, I mean. What cruel things children say to each other, but then, it is only what grown-ups think and say underneath all their little pretenses, don't you think?" Then she laughed.

"Oh, but I'm being too serious, I know. Allow me to call you Tawny. You are certainly different from the Miss Butler that my brother informed me who was to be my companion. Your family, he said, were our neighbors for hundreds of years, those Butlers who were practically our enemies over the border into Cornwall. Butlers Reach. I do confess I don't remember even the name Butlers Reach, and that goes to show you I was hardly ever down in Devon at our manor." She seemed to want to make an effort to have an easy ground between us. "You must drop the *Lady* and just call me Bianca, Tawny. Fancy that we were neighbors and I never knew you existed!"

It made me smile; there was no pretty pretense about her forthright yet refreshing personality. "Then we seem to have suffered much the same lack of knowledge," I said, but didn't add that she was nothing like what her brother had said she was. She moved to the sofa, and I sat down beside her. She suddenly sank back, the burnoose billowing out around her, and she rested her head on the back of the sofa.

"To be honest, I am utterly exhausted, Tawny," and she seemed breathless. "My journey from Kabul to Rawalpindi was hazardous, to say the least. I should not want to attempt it again, and from Rawalpindi over the Himalayas to here has just about done me in. I seem to be quite faint. Not like me at all." She closed her eyes, and I was alarmed.

But before I could say anything, she opened her eyes and said quickly: "You must not breathe a word of this to Toby! He is an old uncle, gruff but harmless, I know. Yet he will carry me off and plunk me down into that tight little British society at Nedou's Hotel and let all the old frumps fall over their skirts to make Lady Bianca Harding as miserable as they are themselves! And I should hate that." She laughed, and I noticed for the first time how flushed she seemed. She brought out a small ivory fan and began fanning her face.

"Perhaps you are momentarily suffering from the altitude, Bianca. Remember, we *are* living in a mountaintop atmosphere even in the Vale of Kashmir; it takes a bit of getting used to. I should think a few days of complete rest would do wonders, and I want to invite you to stay at my house, beginning today. No Nedou's Hotel for you."

She looked at me over the edge of her fan, her eyes dilated almost to a dark stormy blue, and her face blanched, the flush I'd seen earlier paling. It alarmed me.

But she lifted her head and said with a smile, "There. Now that does show you just how little I know of you! I had no idea that you have a house here in this incredible hill station, nor indeed, do I know why you are living in Kashmir! Oh, undoubtedly I shall discover that answer, and we've loads to learn of each other, haven't we? You are most generous and gracious to offer me lodging . . . but how I chatter! You will tire of me easily, I am sure. Oh. Here is dear Toby. Please say nothing, I beg you."

She had already won me over, and I felt things were smoothing out. The fact that her brother had reminded her of my family status with their family left no doubts in my mind about what he had concluded in his own mind of my station in life. He had been wrong about his sister, and this satisfied me beyond expectations, and I was determined to show the man up, when I met him!

Mr. Roberts came into the room with Samsar Koul following him, and two young houseboys bearing huge platters of steaming food, which they placed on the table, and they ran to fetch more throughout the entire meal.

It was a Persian feast, and one of the best I'd ever eaten outside of Mohammud Gulag's cuisine at my table. It was pilaf; shredded mutton stuffed with spices, onions, raisins, pine nuts and oranges; roast kid and fish stuffed with rice and peppers; apricots stuffed with almonds and walnuts soaked in honey.

The chapati, a crunchy flat bread made of coarse wheat flour and baked in clay ovens over charcoal, was used as scoops to eat the pilaf. We used our fingers, simply breaking the chapati into chunks and wrapping it about the rice and mutton and vegetables and eating it.

It surprised each one of us to see that we all had acquired the art of eating in this fashion, a rule unspoken that it was best to join in the customs rather than fight them, and we laughed as we dipped our fingers into the water bowls placed for our use by Samsar Chand Koul, and used the white linen cloths that were none too clean for drying.

Through it all, Bianca was content to make things easy for Tobias by chattering lightly, and we compared our experiences in adjusting to a different culture.

When the plates were removed and the hot, sweet-spiced

Kashmiri tea was brought in, we began to discuss just what and where we'd go from here. Bianca seemed to want to discuss openly what her brother had in mind for her, and she did not hesitate to assure us both that she knew he did not want her to get in touch with David Markus. I met Tobias's eye and knew that he'd been partially correct about her. She wanted her brother to care about her. I was moved.

"It's very simple," she began to explain herself. "David didn't show up, that's all. I thought—well. I believed he would be here, you see. There was no message, and after all I've been through—" She stopped, biting her underlip, and it was an uncomfortable moment for all of us. Tobias said nothing, but I could see he was in deep thought.

I was silent, digesting what she was getting across to us. She had arrived in the Persian Gulf, hoping he would meet her, but this David Markus had stood her up there, and she had traveled to Kabul with other English travelers who had been on her ship. Now she was ready to accept what seemed her destiny.

"So. The sensible thing to do now, since I am here, is to abide by Gordy's wishes. I must confess"—she smiled, her lips pouting prettily—"I have wanted an excuse to go to Nepal. Gordy would never ever have invited me there had I not forced my presence here in India. Admit it, Toby. You know Gordy better than I do. He has never had the slightest intentions of having me live with him anywhere."

In that confession, I believed I heard the plaintive cry of a young girl wanting to be needed by this brother she seemed to admire deeply, and trying to get his attention. She had an adoring fixation, and I felt I could understand. It had taken a great crisis in my own life to bring about the attention I'd needed and wanted from my own father, whom I had admired above all others. I thought I saw it all too clearly in that moment.

Toby's eyes were cool and blue as he studied Bianca, and his answer was dignified. "We must be fair, Lady Bianca. Your brother has always had your interests at heart. He also has the tremendous responsibility of his position to consider, and it demands his undivided attention. But you have been his one great concern through it all. I believe he will be happy to have you with him in Kathmandu."

Tobias Roberts could not be bought with any price. How loyal he was to Lord Gordon Harding! It angered me, but at the same time I had to admire him for it.

Bianca did not blink an eyelash at that; not even one word of reproach about her brother left her lips, and because of this it was much later that I knew it was this fact alone which gave me the sense of uneasiness that did not leave me. However, in that moment, Bianca could not have been more affable to her brother's demands.

We fell into a silence for a short while; the sun made patterns on the balcony with the willow green, and splashes of scarlet and orange marigold lay hot in pools of brightness on the old wooden floor. Inside, the blue and rose of the carpet which covered the room's floor were soft colors, and it was cool and shadowy in spite of the tremendous heat of the sun outside. The muted sounds of the house beyond seemed far away, and stuffed as we were with the dinner we'd had, it all seemed to lie heavy and made a somnolent hour.

"Tawny has invited me to stay at her house, Toby," she said in a languid voice, not at all hurried. I was pleased that it was she who had mentioned the subject. "And I have decided to accept it and with pleasure." She turned to me. "Tawny, dear. I shall move in tomorrow with your approval. That will give me time today to simply relax, I think. Is that too soon?" She lifted her brows and I fancied that I saw a high flush on her cheeks.

"I was expecting that you might come home with me today, Bianca. I mean that. Won't you change your mind and come this afternoon? I can wait, for I have nothing too demanding." I meant it sincerely.

Toby picked up my defense. "Of course you must go with Miss Butler, Lady Bianca. This place is not fit for you to remain in. It is not safe, either. There are known cases of women being kidnapped in broad daylight by some of these caravan drivers. They know what price a white woman can bring on the slave trade markets! You are probably the most watched young woman ever to have crossed these premises. You must change your mind, and let me take you back to Miss Butler's house."

She looked aghast, then burst out laughing. "Oh, Toby! For a moment I thought you were serious. I am perfectly safe here. I have Samsar Chand Koul eating out of my hand, as well as the houseboys. No one could be more safe than that!"

"My dear Lady Bianca! You are an heiress, and therefore worth a ransom! I feel it my duty to remind you that should word ever get about that you are an heiress, your life would be very much in danger. And heaven help the scoundrels if Lord Gordon should catch up with them!"

Her soft laughter mocked his seriousness. "That would be most exciting, I must admit. Kidnapped and held for ransom by one of those tall dark-eyed Kirghiz chiefs, hidden in a caravan, and Gordy so angry that he'd come out of his shell to rescue me! How romantic! It does appeal to my imagination." She was dreamy-eyed for a moment, in a cloud of romance, and for one brief second it occurred to me that she could be the sort of fanciful girl to attempt to jeopardize herself just to get the attention of her brother. I shivered inwardly.

"It does have all the romance of a novel," she went on, seeing the expression on Toby's face, and when I said nothing, she added, "but I fear my brother's wrath more than my love for that kind of adventure." I thought then that she might have changed her mind about coming with me today.

"I won't be persuaded to move from my lodgings this day, dearest Toby. Tawny. You must help me convince him that I am perfectly safe for now. If I haven't been kidnapped by those brigands of Persia and Afghanistan whose caravans I passed daily for the past six months, then one more night will scarcely find me in the snatches of a bloodthirsty Mongolian driver!" She stood up. "No. I shall remain here, because I want to rest. I will arrive on your doorstep with bag and baggage tomorrow, Tawny." This was not an unprotected little girl speaking, but a young woman with a mind of her own, and I heard the hard flintlike determination in every word. It was her way too, of dismissing us, and there was nothing else we could do but to accept it.

"Very well, then, Lady Bianca." Toby's voice was even and revealed only his polite concern. He would not argue. He stood up as I did, and became all protocol and official. "We shall leave you here, trusting that you will keep your doors locked, and a servant to sleep across the threshold of your room. Don't forget that most important measure of safety. Give me your word on that score, and I shall rest easier on leaving you in this place."

I was suddenly amused by it all. She was right, of course. She had proved that she could think for herself, and there was no need to be alarmed. She was perfectly safe, even as safe as I was in my house above the lake. Hadn't she even proved it by being here last evening? And she was right about the proprietor, Samsar Chand Koul. He was eating out of her pretty little hand. I knew a word with him from Tobias Roberts would put him straight. He would turn the house upside down to protect her.

"Of course I will give you my word, Toby dear. You have it. My servant always sleeps across the doorway, with a knife in his hand. Be easy in your minds, both of you." She smiled, rather wanly, and touched my arm gently. "I am looking forward to tomorrow at your house, Tawny. We have much to talk over."

"Then it will be my pleasure to have you there. Take care, Bianca. I shall expect you." I gave her instructions on how to find the house.

We left her then, Toby and I, with our last glimpse of her going up a flight of dark wooden stairs to where her rooms were. I knew Toby would have liked to follow her up those stairs simply to check on all safety measures, but he did not do so.

He did not return to my house with me afterward, but left me in the care of his driver, saying he had an important engagement which must be kept. It was understood that he would pay a call in a few days' time to see how well we fared, and he stood in the sun, his hand lifted in farewell as the carriage rolled away from the chenar-lined street in front of the residency.

4

I was restless, haunted by my thoughts that evening, as I sat out on my porch. The garden was heavy and sweet with the bright hot summer flowers of marigolds and zinnias. It seemed to me that all the summer colors had grown richer each day, and even the tall gold sun daisies shone like balls of gold. On that summer night, the garden smelled of petunias too, and there was a scent of dog roses and of hay flowers from the canal fields where Mohammud's family had been cutting the late hay for weeks now.

The sound of music on the drums and sitar played by the old country musician who had come down from the hills to stay in the village just below Gulag's house, filled the night with sad, haunting tunes in a minor key. He sang in a voice that was strangely sweet and thin and unbearably sad. I'd seen him on several occasions; he had a white beard that matched his long hair, and he seemed older than anyone I'd ever met before. His face held an emaciation that was dark and noble, and his singing held the attention of everyone who listened.

The night was deep with stars, and a moon climbed in a velvet sky. Old memories had been stirred inside me, and when I finally retired to bed, sleep was a long time in coming. I could not throw off those memories, and when I did fall into a restless sleep, I dreamed again that old dream which had often been a nightmare in those first years after the terrible crisis in my young life eight years before.

When I awakened to find it was still night, I could not help my thoughts, and so I just let them come; as if winding a skein of colored wool into a firm ball one more time, my mind went over it all again.

Certainly, Sir Lyle and Lady Gillian Pearson had not treated me unkindly, although at the end, when it all came to a dramatic climax, I had believed them to be the most hardhearted Christians in the universe. That I had been a friend of their handicapped daughter in our school years, in that fashionable London school for young ladies which my father had placed me in, had endeared me to them. They had invited me to stay with Sarah in their large house beside the Thames in Twickenham when I left school and while my father was in India.

But how could they have known just how fallible their own son was—he who they believed was a saint? Neil had come home from Oxford, a promising young man of twenty-three destined to follow in his successful father's footsteps. I know I fell in love with this brown, almost golden-eyed man, whose hair and beard had that golden sheen like a young King Midas, and I fell under his charm. But I had believed he loved me too, and that was why I could give myself to him so completely.

What I didn't know until it was all too late, was that Neil was engaged to be married; there was the ball, and the stunning announcement of the wedding to take place very shortly. Blind to all of this, I knew without a doubt that it was I whom Neil loved, and before the ball when he seduced me, I had believed he would throw off the lie and would marry me instead of Lindsey Ash.

I was wrong, of course. He married Lindsey in a great splash of publicized grandeur. Nothing but the best for Neil Pearson; he had been loved all his life. He had been adored by every female from his cradle to manhood; even women dottering with age adored Neil. His sister, Sarah, had worshipped him.

I had remained in the Pearsons' home, absolutely crushed; I wanted to rush down to Cornwall and die, but because Sarah clung to me like a leech and pleaded with her parents to keep me from leaving at any price, I stayed. How could I have been so blindly in love with him? It took my breath away even now. I had been a woman on fire.

During that year, Sir Lyle and Lady Gillian went on a six-month cruise down the Nile in Egypt, leaving Neil and Lindsey in charge of the house, and Sarah in my company. Later I thought I might be pregnant and I became distraught about the prospect of such a situation. Somehow, Sarah had discovered that I'd had the affair and I believe it was she who told Lindsey everything.

Possessive and cunning, Lindsey Ash Pearson knew she could never hold on to her beautiful husband, but when she discovered his infidelity, her diabolical mind spun into orbit. She laid her plans well.

"I am your friend, Tawny Butler," she said, coming to me. "Believe me. I want to help you. But we must not let Sir Lyle and Lady Pearson, nor even Neil, guess the truth. Let me take care of all the arrangements. Trust me to do the right thing." I could not let my father know I was a fallen woman and could possibly be carrying an illegitimate child. Nor did I dare let Neil find out. So I decided to let Lindsey help me, if necessary. She outlined plans to find a cottage with a maid for me to live in until the baby came. She also began to press me about possibly giving up the child since I was a single woman but I was too distressed to even think clearly about that.

As it turned out, I discovered that it was a false alarm, and this gave me an uneasy peace. However, Lindsey took the opportunity to vent her full wrath upon me and quickly forced me out of the Pearson house. Distressed and confused, I sought my father's help and I never saw or heard about Neil again.

My father had helped me pick up the pieces of my life after that. He'd been gentle and understanding all the way. My memories of him were ones of love and gratitude, for when I needed him, he'd been there.

*

As the wind rose to a shrill high pitch outside the old Lamaist monastery in the Gurla Mandhata Pass, I shivered down into the fur rug, unable to close my eyes and sleep in spite of the exhaustion from the day that had brought me here.

An icy blast tore down through the skin-covered window slits, chilling the very marrow of my bones. The embers of the fire in the brazier glowed faintly, and I shifted uneasily out of my cocoon of the rug to throw more yak dung on it. Flames leaped at it greedily, and I shivered again in my night shift.

I looked at Chanda, who at that moment I envied because she could drop off from her days of weariness and drift into a blessed state of oblivion. I went over to her bed and pulled the rug about her and the sleeping baby and tucked it around them firmly. They did not even stir or sigh. Yes, I envied them both, but I was glad that at least they could do so.

I hurried back to my quilts and wrapped the fur about me again, settling down. Grotesque shadows flickered on the stone walls in wild shapes, disturbing patterns, and the screaming wind was like a trapped animal's death throes.

I would not allow my mind to go ahead of me into the next weeks we had to get through before there could be that relative safety I was seeking for Bianca's little son. No. I shut my mind to it firmly. Too much was unknown, and I would cross those bridges when I came to them.

Why couldn't I shut out the past as easily as that, I asked myself, knowing it was flapping about my mind like a torn, ragged cloak in the wind. How do I begin to explain those incredible events which unfolded on that late but bright August day in my house above Dal Lake, when I expected Lady Bianca to arrive on my doorstep, and she did not, in fact, arrive at all?

I blinked my tired hot eyes in the dark old gompa cell, hoping by doing so to shut out the past, but like those shadows on the wall, flame-lit, those other scenes just seared across my mind unbidden and in full vivid clarity.

*

The lake was a quiet Japanese gray; hardly a sound came up from it, not even the jump of a fish nor the splash of a paddle from one of the flatboats which drifted across its placid surface. The mountains were deep purple, and the peaks were lifted up into a faint swirl of shell-pink mists.

I rose early, restless, though I tried to put from my mind all the past that had been dug out so untimely by Lord Gordon Harding's letter and request of me. I realized, that had he known exactly my own past life and its crushing experience, he would never have chosen me for this task of guiding his wayward sister! And it occurred to me again, what indeed had Lady Gillian written to him about my character that could have been so sterling?

But all that was over and done with, I told myself, and it could alter nothing now. I went out into the garden, and stared at the lake so serene. A new prospect had opened for me, providentially, and I was going to make the best of those changes by forgetting my old griefs.

My dear father had died tragically before I could really prove to him that I had healed under his love and concern for me, and I had mourned this as I mourned him. Then Gavin had given me his special attention, and now he too was gone, but I had survived, and I had to go on living. This new challenge was a bid for that life, and I accepted it.

If Lady Gillian had chosen this time in her life to forgive me, I saw no need to ask questions. There was no real reason to hold on to a grief for someone who was lost to me. Neil had never been mine to lose, not in that sense. And there was no need to remember the dead past.

If I could help Bianca at this time in her life, perhaps I could settle that debt I owed my father, I thought, as I turned and began cutting the fresh flowers I wanted to place in her room, and began to look forward to this day ahead of me, and for Lady Bianca's coming into my life. I was happy.

*

It was late afternoon and she had not arrived. I was not unduly alarmed, but I kept an anxious vigil nonetheless as the hours drifted by. The house looked its most charming, scented with the late roses and with the hot orange and yellow marigolds I'd arranged in great clumps of color throughout the rooms. I was certain she would appreciate it.

At last, I heard the sound of the carriage; it came at a tremendous sound of speed, and I hurried down the stairs and out on the porch just as it lurched to a stop down by the gate.

The latch clicked loudly, like an echo in the hush of the afternoon, and I kept an anxious eye on the garden path that wound under an almond tree. To my dismay, Bianca did not appear, but Mr. Roberts did. I waited, but she was not behind him. As he hurried up the path, I became aware that he was dressed in khaki carefully tucked inside highly polished brown boots for bush riding. He removed his helmet carefully and placed it under one arm as he came up the steps.

Not by any outward emotion did he display what he was feeling, yet I saw the blazing blue of his eyes, and an uneasiness flowed over my heart.

"Is anything wrong, Mr. Roberts?" I couldn't keep the apprehension from my words. "Lady Bianca has not yet arrived. I've been expecting her—"

He lifted his hand in a gesture that he already knew this. "Miss Tawny. The worst has indeed happened. I drew it out of that oily Samsar Chand Koul, by heaven if I didn't! Lady Bianca has disappeared from the inn. It looks like an abduction, from all I can learn. She was taken forcibly, and probably in a small party that is making for Kashgar. Now"—his eyes never left my own—"there isn't time to go into details, but what I want to know is this.

"Will you come with me? I'm going after her. She may need you when we catch up with her abductor. We cannot waste time. I'm heading out this very hour."

We stood on the steps facing each other, and my heart leaped to this invitation, almost staggered with mixed emotions I hadn't even dared dream of.

"Of course I will go with you. I shall consider it my duty. Just give me one moment to prepare—" I stopped, seeing his lifted hand again.

"I've already taken care of our preparations. Our mounts and packhorses are waiting at the crossroads in Gandarbal. We shall make for there immediately. And I shall speak to Mohammud while you prepare yourself. I think your houseboy, Jaseen, should come with us. He can do for you on the trail."

"Very well. I shan't be long."

I hurried to my rooms, changed into my riding clothes, and put together things I felt I should need for some time, and I joined Tobias and Jaseen. Thus, within two hours at sunset, our little caravan of five left Gandarbal heading toward Gilgit, the northernmost outpost of Kashmir, riding hard.

It was one month later, when Toby and I reached Gilgit, that we stumbled upon the whole truth of Bianca's disappearance.

The trail we'd come over had been a rough one, and we lost precious time by following up many false rumors. Toby had been patient, and we both had believed we should find Bianca before winter. We were tracking an enemy who was known to have taken many women to the slave markets in China, but this abductor was elusive even though we felt that we had been very close at times.

Thus, it was at the end of September when we came into Gilgit and took rooms in an old inn near the marketplace. The snows had not yet come, but it was cold. The leaves were brassy bright red on the old chenar trees, and the pine was a thick dense green on the mountain slopes.

We had arrived near midmorning, and I was grateful to be lodged in a room, albeit one bare of furnishings except for a low cot with webbed ropings, a table and one chair. To me it was luxury after living in a tent for four weeks. It was also a good chance to stock up on supplies, and I sent Jaseen out with instructions to find them.

Toby had left me in my room and had gone alone to the marketplace, where the caravans converged, to learn what he could. He returned after a brief hour and informed me of the news. I gave him a bowl of salted yak-butter tea as he sat down on the chair, and I returned to the cot, where I sat cross-legged on a quilt.

He'd learned that a small caravan led by an English trader known as Markus had come through Gilgit three days ago, on its way to Baltit, the capital of Hunza. A white woman was with him.

I was stunned. I could say nothing even had I wanted to, so I simply stared at Toby, sipping that thick brew. It wasn't hard to figure out that she had deceived us both; that she had arranged the whole abduction plot to look as if she had been forcibly taken, while in fact she had slipped away in disguise and had met up with David Markus as prearranged.

I should have been angry; she'd been deliberately deceptive, with the cunning of a little vixen, and I was reminded all over again that her brother had cautioned me in his letter that she would do this. I could have laughed and passed it off as a great joke, but because Toby was so serious, and watching me, I spoke out my thoughts.

"So it has all been for nothing." My voice was reflective, yielding to defeat too easily. "She set out to deceive us both from the beginning." I wasn't indignant, for I'd been forewarned, but my concern for her welfare had been genuine. "She is already with David Markus, and nothing we can do can alter that."

Toby was quiet, in deep thought, and I knew by his silence that he had more to say, so I waited. We had lived closely during the weeks past, and he had been unrelenting in our pursuit, wild as it had now turned out to be. We'd ridden hard and had camped in primitive overnight places, setting out each day with the sunrise in our faces, with the hope that we'd somehow catch up with the elusive abductor before he could cross the Hunza border into China before the snows came.

I felt I knew Toby as he knew me by now; it had been a curious relationship all the way, and I hadn't minded the harsh demands of such rough travel, not at all. More than once, I was aware Toby had given me looks of appraisal for my perseverance in the thick of it; but it had been a full experience highly incensed by the fear of Bianca's fate in the hands of a slave trader.

It was some long moments before Toby spoke what was on

his mind, and when he did so, I felt I had been too rash, too ready to admit defeat.

"There is news just filtering in from Baltit with the first caravan traders. I can't ignore that news, Tawny. When Markus arrived in Baltit, a Kirghiz chieftain of a Turkistani tribe, known as Khan Shayet, came tearing down into Baltit from the north and confronted Markus. He called Markus out, which meant he wanted a fight. But, apparently, Markus refused and later was reported to have slipped out of Baltit. Rumors have come that he fled, leaving his caravan and the white woman, and that the Kirghiz took her as his captive. I don't like it." He shook his head slowly, staring down into his empty bowl, then lifted his eyes to meet mine. There was a faraway light behind the blue I saw there.

"Do you suppose Markus deserted her?" Even as I said that, I remembered Lord Gordon's prophesy that Markus could not be trusted. I could only speculate in what direction Toby's thoughts were heading.

"I don't know what to think on that score, Tawny. But I don't like the sound of it. That we have virtually no proof, only hearsay, that Lady Bianca is a victim of her own making now, however deserving or not, I cannot allow it to pass without looking into it all fully."

The beard on his face, which he'd let grow during these past weeks, was a deep russet shade next to his sandy hair, and it accentuated the fierce blue of his eyes; they narrowed as a small silence held us, and I waited almost breathless for his next words.

"I am going after her, Tawny. There is little else I can do. It may take weeks, months, and the snows will come. But I am going after her." He was positive, patient beyond all endurance, and loyal to an infuriating degree to Lord Gordon Harding! He stood up, and I saw that strange light in his eyes.

"I cannot ask you to continue on with me, for it is too hazardous, as well as dangerous. I will arrange for you to join a caravan to return to Srinagar—"

"I wouldn't dream of putting you to that task, Toby!" I

cried, and I stood up to face him. "Besides, I feel I must earn that money which Lord Gordon entrusted to me." I laughed. "Where you go, I can go. Bianca will need me. I do insist," I added quietly.

He feigned surprise. "It may be dangerous . . ." he began, then hesitated.

I shrugged. "Bianca is in danger, and far more than I may ever know. She will need me, I'm certain." I was persistent, and as we looked at each other I could see that he was actually relieved as well as pleased.

"Very well, then. That's settled. We may as well move on, and not waste precious time. I believe every hour will count now. We have the weather to fight from here onward."

Preparations had to be done quickly. Fresh mounts were bargained for, and those supplies Jaseen had brought back were stashed in the packs. Toby wrote a letter to Lord Gordon, and I wrote a small note to Jaseen's grandfather, Mohammud Gulag, informing him of our prolonged journey. The letters, once written, went out with the caravan that left shortly after noon heading for Srinagar.

Thus, barely a few hours in Gilgit, our small caravan set out once more on the first stage of our ride into the kingdom of Hunza. Toby had hired a Hunzukut guide to take us along one of the most treacherous trails we had yet to pass over. Jaseen and Gulam, Toby's man from Srinagar, were both able-bodied men who did not hesitate to ride along at a quick pace and who looked after the surefooted animals.

We rode hard and fast along the Gilgit River for several hours. Then, just as the sun was making a red disk of flame between the snow peaks, which always surrounded us in this high country, we rounded a bend sharply to the left and entered into the Hunza Valley. The road began to climb. As it climbed, the trail grew narrower, and rougher than any trail I'd previously known. It was no more than a beaten dusty track of rock worn by hundreds of years over which camel caravans had traveled over from Kashgar to Kashmir.

I marveled at this, for I knew my own grandfather, Sir James

Butler, had traveled over these very treacherous trails, and I was sure Gavin had done so many times too. Every few feet, our horses kicked up rocks and pebbles that were flung out into space, landing in the canyons far below. The trail was but a ledge, not wide enough for more than one horse, single file. Our guide pushed ahead with absolute devil-may-care assurance; he knew every inch of the trail, knew its hazards, but he rode in his saddle with a straight proud back, fearless, and we could do little but follow.

It was already dark when we descended into the floor of the valley and found a huddle of stone buildings that resembled a wayfaring inn for pilgrims, and we were made welcome for the night. The first of the icy winds of late September blew down through that canyon, heralding a winter that was to come all too soon; thus I was glad for the protection of the thick stone walls that night.

The earthen floor was beaten down smoothly around the warmth of the fire pit in the center; it was pleasant and quite comfortable as well as amusing, as we sat around that fire and shared dried apricots and walnuts after our supper of roasted kid, with the members of a passing caravan going south and the owners of the inn.

Toby was anxious to glean any information he could from Baltit, and what the caravaneers had to tell seemed to border on the very worst of our fears. He fell silent, and it was obvious that he was disturbed.

One of the caravan drivers had crudely asked Toby if he had some opium he wanted taken into Kashgar, and through the deep thick haze of smoke in the room I saw Toby's eyes narrow. "Do you make runs with opium?" Toby asked.

The Mongolian driver assured him that he did, for a price. He was just returning from Kashgar, where he had taken the run to his contacts. Toby seemed unusually interested in this illegal trade. I had known about it for some time, for Gavin had told me that the British were involved with transporting it from India into China. That had been just before Gavin's disappearance, so I hadn't learned anything more. But I was thinking about it, and when a lull in the smoky room made everyone drowsy, I asked Toby if he'd known my brother.

- He looked at me in his very quiet manner before answering, seeing that the driver he'd been talking with was now in a dispute with another driver. Toby seemed to be weighing each word carefully as he spoke.

"It would be hard working for Lord Gordon and not know your brother, or about his movements, Tawny. Yes. I knew Gavin. He was the very best of agents, trained in his skill. He will be a hard man to replace."

I swallowed hard. "Lord Gordon seemed to think that—that he just may be alive. Do you share this?" My voice was husky.

He frowned thoughtfully, and began to stuff his pipe with tobacco from a rather small leather pouch he'd brought from his pocket. He didn't speak until he had lit it with a long thick stick jabbed into the fire pit and begun puffing on it.

"I honestly don't know what to think on that score, Tawny. Do you know the circumstances, that is, the work he was involved in when he disappeared?" I shook my head, and he said, "Gavin was often over this trail, for his job was to intercept the illegal runs of opium by our own countrymen. Of course, we're sure David Markus is one of those drug traffickers, long suspected."

I was stunned. My expression must have revealed this, for he said, "Gavin was like his grandfather, Sir James Butler, Tawny. You knew about your illustrious grandfather, didn't you? He was a high-ranking officer in British intelligence, I believe, a man who made his fortune out of his career, if I remember well enough. He lost his life in that strange mishap near Kashgar"— he spoke almost musingly—"the very place where Gavin was last seen on the first of June. I'll admit I am as puzzled as anyone else is out here about just what happened to that brother of yours, Tawny."

My heart took a strange little dip of fear for no reason at all, and I shivered; I had an uncanny sense of foreboding. That Toby knew much about my family which I hadn't known was obvious; had he known about the enmity between the Butlers and the Hardings? About the circumstances which had driven my grandfather to that career of adventure and chance? He spoke of a fortune, but I knew there was very little fortune left of my grandfather's trade and his work in British intelligence.

"I had no idea . . . you could know Gavin so well," I said, then gave a shallow laugh. "Nor did I know that he was involved with the opium traffic—that is, working toward that end," I said hurriedly. "I believed he was an agent—well, in the Ladakhi affair . . ."

"Oh, that was a cover-up, to be sure. The diplomatic agent sort of thing. He was trained for this more dangerous work, and he was one of our best at it. Everyone liked Gavin. I might as well tell you, Tawny, that this whole thing smells all the way through like an opium run, and that somewhere in Kashgar, or even east of it, your brother has come up against a hard-core organization determined to maintain the runs into Peiping and Shanghai. I'm convinced of it." His voice was low, thoughtful. He was not one who spoke out his thoughts too readily. "Markus. If we could just get to him—" He stopped, frowning, and absentmindedly began to fill his pipe again.

I waited for him to go on, but whatever he'd been ready to say, there was no chance he'd do so, for as I glanced around us, other faces and ears were watching Toby and listening, even though very few of those drivers could speak English. It was eerie to say the least.

That night, I was restless and couldn't get to sleep easily, and I was glad when morning came. We left long before sunrise, yet I was anxious to leave the inn. That day, I had my first glimpse of one of the most magnificent mountains I had ever seen, and one which we were to see for many days and weeks to come.

Our guide Mirzah informed us, Rakaposhi, Goddess of the Snows, held her peak proudly against a deep-blue sky. It was an awesome granite pyramid, mantled with snow, an unconquered titan of the Himalayas. Wisps of snow were whipping across its face, foretelling the closing of the passes when snow blocked them for the winter.

But I had little time to reflect on the mountain's magical beauty: Toby was a relentless driver, and we pushed on as if death were after us.

It was near midday of the following morning when, in a sudden turn of the trail, we had our first view of Baltit, a kingdom that was little known to the outside world. In the clean transparent air, the ancient castle towered before us, looking as serene and remote as the giant Rakaposhi behind it.

The last yellowed leaves on the trees in the valley were blown before the clean icy wind that swept down off the mountain, yet even as this wind whirled down in that icy blast off Rakaposhi, whose peak rose in mysterious splendor above the valley, the sun was glittering in an indescribably blue sky.

We stopped to look in wonder at this magnificent scene; it was one of rare beauty, quite like a silk-screen painting. Baltit sat in a broad green valley, with terraced fields down to the banks of the Hunza River. Winter crops had been sown, and the new tender green was like a fine brush across the whole of the valley, with the mystic mountain always guarding it.

Toby was as silent as I was, and had I been inclined to paint, I am certain this was what would have inspired me. I was speechless to this beauty, knowing I was moved deeply by it. I wondered if Toby felt moved too, but when he spoke, it was not of the valley nor of the mountain.

"I must confess that I'm uneasy, Tawny. From what I've been able to glean from those traders in the caravans we passed, the situation doesn't add up to anything except to intense greed. Markus is a fool to have placed Lady Bianca in reach of this Kirghiz chief. I understand that he would have no scruples, none whatsoever, in ransoming Lady Bianca's person for the highest bid. He would cut Markus's throat and think nothing of it—but a white woman!" It was as if he were speaking to himself as he went on.

"We just may have to push on from Baltit today. The border to the north is not far, but if the snows close the Delhi Sang Pass, we stand no chance in rescuing her. I suggest we stop long enough to get fresh mounts and supplies, and per-

haps I'll see the Mir, the King of Hunza. I've heard from reliable sources that he is fond of the English, and he could give us
support, if nothing else."

Even as he spoke, we saw the long-distance runner on the
road below us coming toward us. Toby gave our guide the signal to start our descent into the valley. An hour later, the
runner met us, and he salaamed deeply to Toby, who had ridden ahead. I saw them in conversation, and when I rode up beside Toby, he said, "We are to go to the castle. It seems as
though the Mir has been expecting us, and he has some important information. I don't like it. Someone from Gilgit must
have known about our plans, and hurried to the Mir with
them. This changes things."

His words struck a foreboding to my heart as our small caravan set out on the last mile before we reached the approach to
the old fortress above the Hunza River.

5

The Mir of Hunza himself greeted us. He was a short man, squarely built, with dark hair and eyes and a ready smile, dressed in a magnificent gown of gold brocade belted at the waist, with a gold-hilted sword in a scabbard of carved ivory at his side. A jeweled pin, surely made of emeralds, held a plume of egret feathers in place on his black hat. It was most impressive, I had to admit, and not at all the fearsome personage I had expected.

Mohammud Jamel Khan, a devout Moslem, ruled all of Hunza, as his ancestors did before him. He spoke flawless English, and received Toby and myself as though we had come as emissaries from Her Majesty the Queen of England, whom he admired so much.

"Welcome to our land," he said politely as he led us into the castle from the courtyard. And no place could have astounded me more, for it was entirely Persian.

He smiled, seeing our expressions when we came into the great hall. It was as though we'd stepped right down into the palace of some medieval Persian prince.

"That is because we are descended from three soldiers of Alexander the Great, who took Persian wives and settled here nearly two thousand years ago." He spoke proudly. "We are a kingdom of great warriors. Even the Chinese empire sends tribute to the Mirs of Hunza to keep us from raiding Kashgar and Yarkand in Chinese Turkistan. But we are a peaceful kingdom too. I want no enemies. My people work and live happily in peacetime." I had to believe him.

As we took our honored places on the deep silk cushions, a

veiled woman came in and sat behind the Mir as incon-
spicuously as she could. She was his wife, the Rani of Hunza.
We were given excellent tea in delicate jade bowls, and only
when the Mir saw that we were enjoying our refreshment did
he speak on the subject which had brought us here.

"One Englishman, David Markus, a merchant trader with a
small caravan passing between India and Sinkiang, was brought
to the castle last evening, Mr. Roberts," he said slowly. "He
will survive from a most severe beating. We have given him
special care. He was incoherent at first, but then he was able to
give me the information that you would be arriving." He spoke
as one detached from the ordinary trivialities of common trade
among the passing caravan traders. He was to be admired for
this, I thought, disturbed by this turn of events.

So, David Markus knew we were following him. I glanced at
Toby to see how he'd received this piece of information. But
Toby did not give one look that would betray any emotion he
felt at the mention of David Markus. He only inclined his head
slightly to one side, and waited in polite dignity to hear all of
what the Mir had to say.

"As a rule, I ignore the caravans who must pass through our
land. I turn a blind eye, as well as a deaf ear, to the market
squabbles among the caravaneers and traders. They have many
old scores to settle among them, rival trains that hold grudges
of some trivial matter. I do not interfere, for it is not good pol-
icy. How they settle it among themselves is not my affair. As
long as they pass through and do not involve or bring harm to
my people, they are welcome to Baltit. We are a peaceful kingdom, but we know how to defend ourselves. We have no pris-
ons, and therefore, we have no prisoners. I await your instructions, Mr. Roberts."

It was astonishing just how he managed to convey there had
been some crucial fight between the Englishman and a man he
did not mention the name of; it was a wise yet uninvolved ver-
dict of a man who must not take sides on outside squabbles,
bur a warning that our countryman was to be placed in our
hands now.

Toby did not bat an eyelash. He inquired after the Kirghiz chieftain. Was he the man the Englishman had come to blows with? To this, the Mir inclined his head and with a smile said politely, "Yes. We understand that Khan Shayet was the man responsible for Mr. Markus's discomfiture. As far as I am able to judge, Khan Shayet left yesterday heading north toward the Delhi Sang Pass, and seemed to be in no particular rush to leave Hunza. He took Mr. Markus's small caravan, which I am to believe the squabble was all about in the first place."

Toby took his time, then he said, "We are here because we have information that a white lady, who was with the Englishman Markus, was taken captive by the Kirghiz chief. She is a close relation to Miss Butler." He gestured toward me, and I had to appreciate the lie. "We fear for her life. If she is harmed in any way, I assure you that Her Royal Highness, our Queen, will be apprised of this matter. If you can give us information about this matter, I shall be obliged. We must rescue her from this notorious bandit before he crosses into Sinkiang."

It was a veiled threat, although Toby did not rise to anger. The Mir sat in a most comfortable golden thought. He seemed under no threat, but I believed that he liked the mentioning of the English Queen, whom he so admired.

It was just like Toby not even to mention David Markus or how Markus knew we were here in Hunza. He was diplomatic all the way, allowing the Mir to see it was the white woman we had come to rescue, and gave the impression at the same time that he would deal with our own national. Perhaps the Mir was under the impression that we might have been business partners of Markus's. But Toby was not wasting time on anything but what we came for.

The Mir merely smiled. "Then we shall discover together what is being said and what has indeed happened to the white woman." He clapped his hands, and a servant came immediately, kneeling at his side. The Mir spoke quickly in Urdu, and after giving the man full instructions, the servant rose, salaamed deeply to his master as well as to Toby, then turned and ran out of the hall.

The Mir turned back to us, smiling serenely. "Baltit has many distinguished guests from time to time. My ancestors enjoyed keeping a record of such guests, and I, therefore, adhere to this age-old custom. It would pleasure me if you both would affix your signatures in our book."

When a servant brought the great gold-edged book, I was not prepared for what the Mir said then. "Miss Butler. In my father's time, a very distinguished Englishman arrived in Baltit in Her Majesty's service. His name was Sir James Butler. Are you, perchance, of the same family? I was a lad then, and I seem to detect a strong resemblance."

"Why . . . yes," I answered, astonished. "Sir James . . . was my grandfather." I could not hide my pleasure, and the Mir turned the pages back to where the signature was carefully penned in flowing writing. The date was the year 1800, the year my own father was nine years old.

"Then my pleasure is doubled, Miss Butler. I remember your grandfather, because I wanted to be like him. That is why I was determined to speak English. And Sir James recommended an excellent tutor who came to Baltit and taught me all he knew. I was rewarded by knowing Sir James."

I was overwhelmed, and even when I signed my name, I thought of my illustrious grandfather sitting in this same room where I sat now, a young man then, no older than Gavin, if that. I wanted to ask the Mir if my brother too, had ever been his guest, but Toby caught my eye, and it was as if he were sending a message to my mind. Say nothing. The moment passed while Toby signed his name, and then the Mir said, "You will want rooms, Miss Butler. It will be a few hours before we can have word, and until then, I would have you make yourself comfortable. When you are relaxed, Mr. Roberts will come for you, and two hours before sundown we shall have a special entertainment which you both are invited to attend. Please allow my servant to show you the way."

"Thank you, Your Highness," I said. "You are most gracious." Toby stood up and helped me to my feet. "Rest as well as you can, Tawny," he said in a low voice close to my ear. "I want to talk with Markus, and then set out as quickly as possible. I'll come for you." I nodded and then followed the servant who was waiting for me.

From the corner of my eye, I noticed that the Rani, her bright-pink silk veil like a mist floating around her, had risen; she did a feminine salaam to her lord and husband, then slipped from the room in another direction, making no sound whatsoever in those strange leather shoes with curled-up toes.

*

I gave myself up to the moment at hand, and made use of the luxury I'd been denied for weeks, and which the pretty maids of Hunza's generous Mir brought me. Hot scented water in a huge copper tub to sink my whole body into, and while I soaked, they took my clothes away to clean.

I tried not to dwell on the sense of foreboding uneasiness that hovered about me; it was relaxing to lather my skin with the lavender soap I brought out of my pack, and to rinse it off with hot water and plenty of it. I let my tense mind just flow with the steam and the soap, but even so, I thought of Bianca.

It was true I hadn't had much time to dwell on the indignant jolt I'd felt when I learned of her deception. Because she had seemed the innocent victim of her brother's vicious, hard-hearted assessment of her character, I had blindly trusted her. But her deception had backfired, and it was no use in accusing her now. I wanted to help her out of this bad situation, even if it meant that she would be united with her lover and not go to her brother. I wanted to remember the impetuousness of her youth above all.

When I stepped free of the bath and rubbed my body dry with a thick clean towel, I was given an elaborate silk and soft wool costume to wear: pantaloons that billowed out under the warm tunic of soft cream cashmere, stitched in fine embroidery and trimmed elaborately with fur. A pale lemony green silk scarf attached to a small yellow velvet hat which sat on my head, swathed about my face and hair in a gauzy effect. I felt as

though I had stepped back into a sultan's harem when I saw
my reflection in the mirror.

I had time now to study the room I had been given; it too
was very seductive; rich brocaded silk hung from ceiling to floor
over the walls, and Persian carpets thick and glowing in stunning colors covered the floors. Every conceivable pattern and
color was in those carpets, and they stirred all that poetry and
romance I'd felt when I first came into the Himalayas.

I thought of my grandfather again; of course, he'd been here
many, many times after that recorded visit he'd made. I remembered that Grandfather had once taken me on his knee
when I was about eleven, a year before his death, and had told
me of these faraway kingdoms on the top of the world. I hadn't
known him very well at all, to tell the truth, but the few times
I'd seen him down at Butlers Reach in Cornwall had been impressive ones and had imbedded him in my memory firmly as a
great hero.

I couldn't throw off the growing sense of uneasiness, however, and I went to the balcony, which opened out from a parapet, and gazed out over the mellow scene of a hazy golden afternoon that stretched out from mountain to mountain. Yet
for all the beauty and romance in this strange and magical
land, I knew it could be cruel. People lived close to the earth,
simple and practical for survival, striving with their animals to
whip the famines, the elements, the epidemics and the warlords
who waged constant wars on tiny kingdoms like Hunza.

Had Gavin been here too, perhaps under an assumed name?
The Mir seemed to have an eye for family resemblances. Yes,
Grandfather and I did have the same Butler coloring, and it
was true our eyes were shaped much the same. But Gavin? No,
I thought. There was very little resemblance between us.

A shiver of apprehension made goose pimples stand out on
my arms, as questions reared up in my mind. Why had the Mir
been interested in saving the life of David Markus, one of the
many notorious merchant traders with small caravans who
came through Hunza regularly? Normally, he would turn his

back and let things work out for the drivers as they fell. So why David Markus?

Because the Mir had sent his servant out to learn of the whole affair, where, I could only suppose would be the market-place in Baltit, I knew he would not dare return until he'd found out all the facts.

Yet I was puzzled. The Mir had said the Kirghiz chief had left only yesterday for the north, but that he'd been in no par-ticular rush to leave Hunza. What lay behind that fact? And surely, if David Markus knew that the Kirghiz had taken Bianca captive, why hadn't he insisted upon the Mir's knowing it and pursuing her?

As I stood there with these thoughts and unanswered ques-tions, I heard someone enter the room behind me and I turned. It was Toby, and like a fresh breath of that almost frosty air, he came over to where I stood. I saw at once that he too had been given time to have a bath and now wore a clean shirt and jacket.

"Tawny. I have just been to see Markus." He spoke with a deliberated dislike toward the man. "His injuries are not seri-ous. Bruised more than anything, but no bones are broken, as far as he knows. He took a beating, but by gad, he deserved one for jeopardizing Lady Bianca as he has done!"

I waited, for I could see he had much on his mind. That he believed Markus had sold Bianca out in an act of cowardice had been evident by the way he'd been talking, and it was what I'd feared too. "Did he . . . say what . . . happened?" I finally asked.

"He asked to see you, Tawny. He knew we were coming, and it was as I suspected. Someone in Gilgit had known of our in-tentions and came ahead of us. Spies are everywhere." He smiled, but there was no warmth in it, as he leaned against the parapet on the balcony. The late sun's golden rays touched his beard, glinting off it. He sighed heavily, a frown between his brows.

"I have a nasty little suspicion that all this was planned, set up, like a trap, and I don't like it. I distrust Markus more than ever. Lady Bianca is in the hands of that cutthroat Kirghiz because he had no regard for her safety or her person, to my way of thinking, but it was done for a peculiar reason, and I am not yet certain just what that reason is.

"Markus told me that he did not know what happened; he hadn't wanted to have anything to do with Khan Shayet, and went out of his way to avoid him. He said they were suddenly attacked, and that he was knocked unconscious and kicked around some. When he regained consciousness, someone had carried him to the castle and thus he came to the Mir's attention. Of course, now he knows Lady Bianca is Khan Shayet's captive, for the Mir's servant returned with the facts."

"So he didn't desert her, as we feared?" But my heart sank with fear.

"I'd say it was a good case of desertion, but then, I am being unjust, because I am thinking of her situation, not his. He seemed far more anxious for that damned caravan of his than for Lady Bianca. He even tried to convince me that she would not suffer badly at the hands of Khan Shayet. That is why he wants to talk with you, Tawny."

"Of course. I'll see him. But have you any idea of why Khan Shayet took Bianca captive, if not to use her, or to barter her for a ransom?" I was puzzled, for I did not yet see clearly what Toby suspected.

He was quiet, but his eyes like his beard were glinting in the light. "If I don't miss my guess, Tawny, I'd say we are all being drawn to the Kirghiz, with Lady Bianca as the bait. It's that simple, but I don't quite know just why. But I'll soon find out if I have to throttle Markus's neck, damn him!"

Again, some chilling foreboding brought goose pimples to my skin. Before I could say anything, however, Toby reached out and took my hand, pulling me to him. "We are leaving here in a few hours, Tawny. The Mir has offered us a small party of his men, and we're riding out after Lady Bianca. Markus insists on coming with us. Personally, I don't think he is up to it. But he deserves to suffer in no little way for having brought her to this."

I was surprised that he kept his hand on mine; it was big and warm and comforting, yet I was blushing like a schoolgirl. But he went on talking.

"It will be dangerous, Tawny my girl. The Mir has offered you sanctuary here in his castle. I believe he is quite impressed by your being the granddaughter of his hero!" He laughed. "But seriously, I believe you should remain here. I would feel better about it—"

I held up my hand and moved out of his closeness a short step away from him. "I won't hear of it, Toby. No. I must go with you. There is no question about it, and I'm prepared to do so, dangerous or not. Bianca will need me once we get to her. And I want to be there when she is rescued. I must. Besides, I somehow *know* she can't really be safe with that bandit, not from what I've heard from Gavin. I must be there."

Oh, much later, it was an overwhelming emotion when I thought back to that swift impetuous decision! And I would not allow myself to even suppose what might have been had I not insisted that I go along with Toby and David Markus! But even so, I could not have done otherwise. I wanted go. To stay behind would have meant anxiety for me.

Toby just looked at me with that quiet manner of his, but I was aware of his respect and something else, which brought me pleasure. My own feelings for this man had begun to grow, and in this moment, our feelings seemed mutual and ripe. I read into his look everything I wanted to know.

"You are a courageous woman, Tawny. It's what I expected you to say, and against my better judgment. But"—he smiled suddenly, radiant in the warm light—"I am glad you will be beside me."

He gave me a long slow look, and I suddenly felt beautiful under his gaze, for he noticed the Persian costume I was wearing.

"It suits you, yes. That long tunic is designed for women like you, I think. But the way you walk is very Western and noticeable, but I'm attracted to it."

I laughed, very much pleased. "Perhaps I should acquire a

chedari, one of those long robes which Bianca wore? It would hide me well enough."

"Hmn-mn. Well, it did not quite hide her well enough, it seems, nor would it disguise your exceptional figure, I should think." He moved over to my side, and placed his hands on my arms, pulling me to him. I never knew just how it happened, but in the next instant I was in his arms, and he was kissing my mouth with such tenderness, and then with such sudden and fierce passion, that it surprised me.

When he lifted his head and looked down into my eyes, I read the message I saw in them. "Nor would I ever want you hidden from me, my dear girl. Tawny. I must speak to you about—"

A short loud clap of hands broke us apart, and we turned, almost guiltily, to face a dark-eyed servant in the doorway, and behind him, coming in, was the tall, slender, bearded Englishman. He spoke in quick Urdu to the manservant, who turned and bowed himself out of the room.

The man faced us. "I beg your forgiveness to intrude upon you so untimely. It seems I had to bribe my way into this part of the castle, but I felt it urgent that I speak with you both."

Toby frowned and gestured to him to come out onto the balcony to join us.

David Markus was younger than I supposed he would be, perhaps a year or so younger than myself. He was tall, with a certain lion strength in his slender build, and his hair was black, matching the beard as well as his eyes. There were dark circles around those piercing black eyes, nor did I see any joy light up in them as he shook my hand. His clothes were of Russian style so that he resembled a Cossack.

"Miss Butler. May I say this, that I am most pleased that you have come out here, and in the interest of Bianca? I can't tell you just how relieved I am that you are here. I have no doubts that Khan Shayet is expecting me to come after her. And when we do rescue her, she will be in need of someone like you."

It was a surprising speech, and it moved me. "Then I'm glad to be of such use, Mr. Markus," I said, meeting those dark eyes warily, trying to learn the extent of his sincerity. But I could find no reason to doubt it. "I want to help Bianca in any way I can."

"Thank you for that," he said, almost humbly. We stood on the balcony together, the late afternoon sun thick with motes of dust dancing like gold around us, and there was much speculation among the three of us.

Toby was rather gruff when he spoke. "As our interests lie solely with the concern of Lady Bianca, Markus, it would help matters if you could tell us exactly what it is this Kirghiz chief wants from you so badly that he took your caravan and Lady Bianca, knowing you would come after them? I have no intention of getting involved with illicit merchant trading. My purpose in being here is to find Lady Bianca. And so help me, I want to find her safe."

I couldn't blame Toby. I knew he felt unsure of the situation, and therefore would not trust David Markus. Indeed, if Khan Shayet had the caravan, which obviously was a source of wealth in what it contained, either opium or other illicit goods, why would he be enticing Markus to follow him, using Bianca as the bait, as Toby had suggested?

But Markus was not going to give up his secrets, not that kind and not in my hearing; instead, he gave Toby a knowing look, then in a strange little awkward moment, he said, "I beg you to understand, both of you, when I say this. Bianca is . . . well. She is with child. My child. Four months gone. That is why I must get to her. The Kirghiz chief won't harm her, unless he doesn't get what he wants. But he will use her. Oh, my God, and how he will use her!" The man suddenly lost control and began shaking. His whole body began to tremble visibly, and he could not stop it.

I could have sworn that Toby was about to strike him because his fists were clenched, his face had blanched and his mouth tightened. But Toby was not a man who acted rashly. When his arm reached out and his hand caught hold of

Markus's upper arm, it was I who flinched because of my fear
that he would strike the man.

"Take it easy, old man," he said gruffly, and I knew he was
covering up his own soft heart. I was moved to tears. "Let me
assure you. We are going out after her, and every second
counts."

David stood with his back to the parapet, to brace his shaking body; I could see that he'd truly been beaten, and I suspected he'd lost a great deal of strength.

"Miss Butler. I believe you are the sister to Gavin Butler, are
you not?"

I was taken aback. "Yes. Of course. Do you know my
brother?" I felt as if the breath had been knocked out of me. I
saw Toby tense beside me.

"Yes. I know your brother. He goes under an assumed name,
but nevertheless I am well acquainted with him. I suppose I
would be a very wealthy man by now, if it weren't for Gavin
Butler!" He smiled then, but it was a mock smile.

Every nerve inside me was pulsating; I wanted to find out if
he knew Gavin's whereabouts, but I had a warning look from
Toby. David steadied himself, and the trembling of his body
ceased. He took a great deep breath, his hands pressed hard
against the stone wall.

"God, if I only knew what happened to him! Everything
depended on his being where we planned to meet! I am sure
the Kirghiz is responsible, and this—all this is his way of drawing me to his camp on the Little Pamir. I know he is heading
there. We must try to get to them before the snows start, Roberts." He turned to face a steely-eyed Toby. "Once the snows
come, Delhi Sang Pass will bar us from our return or prevent us
from getting to Bianca."

I was surprised; that Gavin was involved with Markus as well
as the Kirghiz chief seemed almost ludicrous, especially after
the praises sung by Toby that my brother had been above all
this!

But Toby said, "Then I suggest that we go to my rooms. I
have some brandy that will steady you. We'll need you along to

guide us, Markus." He looked at me. "Tawny. Have all your things readied. I'll come back in a short while, and we'll go to see what the Mir has planned for us. But afterward, we shall depart."

When they left me, I knew I was disturbed more than ever, and restless. So much was on my mind. I felt certain that Toby had been about to speak his heart to me before Markus interrupted us. I knew, too, that I would have answered him truthfully. But the words had not been spoken, just as if fate had intervened.

I didn't allow my thoughts to dwell on this pleasant hope, knowing we should be together for many days and hours, and our feeling toward each other would have more than enough time to grow. Words didn't need to be said, I knew.

My thoughts went to Bianca. She was pregnant, and in the hands of that renegade Kirghiz. A cold hand clutched at my heart as I thought of her plight. Oh, she had been sly and had fooled Toby and me, but all that I could forgive and I did. It was because I was remembering what I had felt when I thought I was pregnant with Neil's child eight years before that I could understand what she must be feeling. Certainly I wanted to be able to stand beside her when her brother had to be faced and told, and I would not let her down.

Perhaps David Markus did love Bianca; certainly he seemed genuinely anxious for her. But with that love, he should never have jeopardized her safety.

What wild and reckless dreams she had to have to follow this one man out on the highroads of adventure along the old silk and spice routes over the Himalayas! But then, my own grandmother had done the same, and I even thought of my mother, who had traveled alone across the Syrian deserts to meet my father, and had been lost in a caravan for months before Father had rescued her!

In Bianca's case, was David Markus worth it? But then, I couldn't answer that with an unbiased opinion. I knew that I was going out after her, and that nothing would have kept me back now. If Toby was with me, I knew we could not fail to find her. Lord Gordon's trust in Toby was grounded. Toby would not fail, and I would have staked my life on this fact.

The maids entered with my clothes, which they had taken to clean for me. Although it had been only a few short hours, my homespun skirt and shirts, with the underskirts as well, were freshly laundered and ironed. It pleased me so much that I searched around in my pack for three small cakes of lavender soap and gave them each one. They giggled and smiled with delight. I laughed with them.

I set about to change my costume for my own thick tawny-colored homespun skirt and the shirt, tucking it into the waistband neatly, and then pulled on the soft leather boots. As I did so, I was surprised when I glanced up to see the Rani, the Mir's lovely wife coming into the room, with her maid following the billowing cloud of pink veil. Behind that veil, she was smiling, and I stood up to meet her, bowing even as she bowed politely, then waved to her maid to come forward.

In her arms she carried a lovely soft suede fur-lined tunic, deep-brown leather so soft to the touch it was like silk, fashioned to be worn over my clothes as a long coat.

"You will need warmth," she said proudly in a few chosen words of English, surprising me. "The Mir of Hunza, as well as the Rani"—she bowed her lovely shining black-haired head gracefully, indicating herself—"wishes you to have this. It will be very cold where you go. Please."

Astounded, I could only lift the lovely tunic coat, which was lined in thick fur. With it was a fur hat of some light-tawny shade of the tunic's fur. She proudly watched my every movement. I was stunned, for it was the most incredibly luxurious gift I'd ever received from anyone.

Because she waited with such expectancy, I slipped it over my clothes to find that it did indeed fit my figure as if it had been made especially for me. Then I stood in front of the mirror and placed the hat on my head, setting it down with much show, which delighted the maids and the Rani. The hat was beautiful, and behind me were great sighs of pleased admiration and laughter.

I could see that the Rani was eyeing my old cloak. I had hung it upon a hook when I first arrived, and now, impulsively, I brought it to her and asked if she would like to try it on. It was of dark-green wool, lined in yellow silk.

Nothing could have pleased her more; it was English-made, heavy, warm and with a hood. When her maid helped her into the cloak, we both stood in front of the mirror admiring ourselves and preened like peacocks, and I started to laugh. It was a marvelous moment, and one I shall never forget.

I asked her then if she would accept the cloak as my gift to her. And with this our mutual friendship was sealed.

*

When Toby came for me, I was ready. He saw the tunic and hat, which I wore to the fete the Mir had planned for us to see. I knew he was delighted, for his glance was filled with admiration. "You are beautiful, my dear girl," he said. "I warned you, didn't I? The Mir of Hunza has taken a fancy to you. He will be more than pleased to see you wearing his gift to the Dance of the Warriors." But Toby laughed, and we went out to join the Mir and Rani, and I had to admit that my heart was light.

The drummers and the pipers, with great hide drums and long copper trumpets, sat cross-legged on the field in a semicircle, playing a steady beat that pulsated through my body like the warning of some distant but certain sinister disaster. Their faces were magnificent in the dying red glow of the sun, colorful as were the incredible costumes they wore.

Toby and I sat with the Mir, his Rani, and three of their six children, for his eldest sons were not present; the son here was sixteen, a handsome prince who favored his mother. We were seated on a small but broad terrace overlooking a green field, directly in front of us. This was to be a spectacular sword dance, given twice a year, at seedtime and at the end of harvest.

David Markus was not attending, but I had caught a glimpse of him in the stables a short time before, with Jaseen and Gulam, looking after the horses and pack animals. My own leather pack had been sent down with Jaseen to be looked after. I did not have a chance to ask Toby if David had confided anything to him of my brother. We were the Mir's guests now, and our attention was drawn away from what was closest to our thoughts.

Suddenly, two lines of warriors in brilliant robes of Chinese silk, carrying leather shields and curved swords, rushed out onto the field in a circle, facing each other, leaping and cutting through the air with flashing steel blades, then pairing off, and began a most incredible dance to the frenzied beat of drums and pipes.

In their warlike leaps and shrieks, the dancers were magnificent, precise in every movement of body and form and flashing scimitar. The audience too—the villagers and the castle's staff of servants—were gathered outside to watch them perform this ancient rite, their own excited voices lifted in encouragement, so that the dancers seemed to leap in a more fierce manner and couldn't stop.

For all of its precision and skill, and the beauty of the robes which the dancers wore with pride, and which the Mir informed us had been given to him by the Chinese decades ago, I was glad when the dance was over. I couldn't throw off the uncanny foreboding that the dance was only a harbinger of what we could possibly witness in the wild, remote camp of the Kirghiz. It stirred my blood with unaccustomed excitement and fear, and I knew my own eyes were lit up with that feeling, but it mirrored in Toby's eyes too.

Immediately afterward, there was feasting in the hall. I was famished, and the roasted ibex which had been prepared for us could not have been improved on, with baked apricots and mountains of steaming rice. The hot crunchy chapati in huge round disks were brought in by the dozens, and when I tore mine into chunks, I skillfully wrapped the pieces around the food and scooped it up to my mouth, enjoying every mouthful to the delight of our hostess, who had watched me with sheer admiration.

Finger bowls were brought in, and following this, we were

served a delicate sweet wine, which amazed both Toby and me. The Mir explained that this was Hunza wine, and each Hunzukut family drank their wine in the winter, even devout Moslems such as himself.

David Markus sat with us, quiet and brooding, I thought, but I noticed he had not taken in much food, and he barely sipped on the wine.

Then it was over and it was time for us to take our leave. Standing on the porch in front of the castle in the courtyard, with the Rani behind him, the Mir said graciously, "Come back to us when you have found the Englishwoman. We offer you sanctuary for the winter." He looked at the sky, certain of his prediction. "The snows never fail us, and the passes are always closed. We shall look for you, Mr. Roberts. God go with you in peace."

It was like a final benediction. And I stared around me at the strange bandoleered Hunzukut warriors who were to ride with us as escorts and protection. Could I help the shiver of fear mingled with excitement that rippled along my spine then? We were leaving, it seemed, the last outpost of friendly protection. What lay ahead of us was indeed unknown and fearsome.

6

From that hour, until after we'd crossed the high Delhi Sang Pass in the Karakoram Range and reached the Wakhan Corridor to the gates of China, five long days later, our journey was a nightmare I could never put from my mind if I tried.

Relentlessly our guides pushed us on ahead, stopping every two hours for a thirty-minute break and then moving on again. We had exchanged our horses for yaks, great shaggy beasts with rope reins tied to the rings in their noses. They were clumsy-looking giants, but they walked nearly as fast as the horses, and were far more surefooted in those snowy passes we found ourselves in. I could feel the giant heart of the beast beating under the warm lambskin saddle I rode in.

We followed the Kirghiz chief just as if he were beckoning to us with his finger. It was uncanny to learn that Khan Shayet had waited for us, and that when he knew we were following him, he would give us the slip and go through the Delhi Sang Pass barely a day ahead of us.

The Mir's men were excellent guides, and it was because of their superb knowledge of this high country that our lives were saved; the stops we made, we had to lie down while the tea was made and given to us. The altitude was tremendously high, and my heart seemed to burst with its rapid beating. We lay prone on our backs, and when we were given the yak-butter tea, it revived us so that we could continue onward.

I sensed the urgency of the men to get us through the pass and return; I saw their faces as they looked at the mountains. It was already October, and we would not stand a chance to get back through this sinister and awesome mountain pass before the big snows closed it.

We were through the pass and going down when, during one of the breaks, Toby came to me. "That Kirghiz chief has something up his sleeve, and I don't like the feel of it." He spoke slowly, confidingly. "He's just been baiting us, and I know he means to have us on his grounds before he makes his move. We can't surprise him, for he knows just how far we are behind him. It is uncannily deliberate and cunning of him."

His face was a study in the bright light of the sun and snow; the copper beard glinted, and under the fur hat, his eyes made a mockery of that blue sky.

My heart was still hammering inside me as if it were bursting, although I could breathe easier now. I warmed my hands around the bowl of steaming tea, and watched the steam rise and stand still in the high clear air.

"What do you intend to do, then?" I tried to act calmly.

"I'm not sure. We can't rush them. That would be useless. There are too many of them to our few. But tonight, we shall be within reach of his camp. Markus knows we're that close. Damn him! He's holding back something that I don't know! He is closed up like a clam."

I shivered in spite of myself. "What did he have to say of my brother, Toby? I'm certain that he must know something about Gavin that Lord Gordon might not know. Did he say anything more on the subject?" I was hopeful, I knew that. To know that Gavin was not lying dead somewhere with his throat slit, I would have given much to know.

Toby's eyes held mine fiercely. "Look here, my dear girl. I believe we are on the brink of some rich discoveries we didn't bargain for. If there was a way for your brother to get out of a bad situation, you can count on it, he will have done so. Just remember. I am here with you in any situation. Let's just first concentrate on getting to Lady Bianca and get the hell out of here before it's too late.

"But, my dear girl"—he took a step nearer to me, lowering his voice—"you must promise me to be careful. Whatever you do, stay close to me and be ever so careful. I don't like this situation. It smells too damned like a trap. I shall warn Jaseen to never lose sight of you. If what I think is about to happen, happens, then Jaseen's duty is to get you back to Baltit should the worst happen."

Fear twisted around my heart in a crazy grip of pain. "Toby! Nothing must go wrong. Don't—please don't talk like that—" I could hardly get the words out, my heart and throat constricted so.

He must have seen that in my eyes, for he placed his gloved hand over mine firmly.

"Don't be frightened, my dear girl. I'm being cautious, and it's always best to be prepared for anything. We'll come through it all, if we are prepared for the worst. Believe that." But he didn't smile, and I was not heartened, knowing that he was distrustful of the whole situation.

There was no more time to speak, however, for our guides, bandoleered with rifles on their backs, beckoned to us that it was time to move on.

It was not until we made camp at nightfall within the shelter of an ancient stone-and-mud hut, abandoned by its former tenants, that Toby and David made their plans known to each other and to me. We had reached the narrow Wakhan Corridor that ran between Kashmir and Turkistan, right on the Little Pamir, with Sinkiang a few miles directly east, and where the route wound on to Kashgar. But across the already frozen Panj River was the winter camp of the Afghani Kirghiz tribe of nomads, and Khan Shayet's bandits.

David Markus had kept his own counsel during the five days we'd been out of Baltit. That he was suffering a strange torment within himself, I had no doubts; he was like a man possessed to get to that camp across the Panj, and he had often been surly when our guides made us stop. This night he was no different. He and Toby quarreled hotly over their plans.

We were seated around the fire pit in the small mud-walled room, chewing on the walnuts and dried fruit which had become our staple diet, and the inevitable strong yak-butter tea warming us. The Mir's men, all five of them, had remained out in the open with the animals, and Jaseen was cracking walnuts on a slab of rock, while Gulam was threading a large needle to stitch up a broken saddle strap.

Toby and Markus sat cross-legged across the pit from each other, while I was almost drowsing, staring into the flames. Toby stuffed tobacco into his pipe, plainly ready to talk sense into the younger man's plan of stealing into the camp that night.

It began to snow without warning; big flakes came down through the opening in the roof, and sputtered and sizzled on the crackling logs. It was like a warning; for a stunning long moment, no one spoke, but I saw eyes meet eyes, and I knew they too knew we had no time to lose, but had to act tonight if we had any hopes of getting back over that route we'd just crossed.

Toby's eyes narrowed as he carefully lit his pipe. But it was David who spoke his mind.

"I will go alone," he said darkly, his black eyes strangely still in the flickering yellow light. "When the hour grows late, I will go. I will have less chance of being seen then. There's no need for both of us to enter Khan Shayet's camp."

"You're mad," Toby said. "It's unthinkable. I haven't come this far to make a bungled-up rescue. No. We've got to have a sound and reasonable plan. It's a trap set up, and he's no fool. Even if you went in there, what good would that do in releasing Lady Bianca? Our cause would be lost." He puffed on the pipe, and he fell into deep thought.

The fire flickered and cast a garish yellow color on the smoke-blackened walls of the hut; logs snapped loudly, and in spite of my drowsiness, I kept awake. I poured more tea from the heavy brass samovar into the empty bowls and passed them around again.

Toby said suddenly: "Where do you reckon he will have placed her?"

"There's no doubt about that. She'll be in the big yurt with all his women. It will be the largest one. They keep in there for warmth."

"Then, damn it! We'll have a hard time of getting her out without attracting attention. So we must distract the whole damn camp in some unforeseen plan." He continued to frown, leaning forward slightly, his face a study of calculation.

David spoke then, very quietly, and made his point. "There is one way, if I can make you see the reasoning in it. I will distract their attention, Roberts, in order to give you enough time to get into that yurt where she is. But you'd have to act quickly; even that would be risky, for she could be bound, and some of those women inside would be guarding her, and they can fight like devils being freed.

"But however you look at it, it's going to be a touch-and-go thing. It's me Khan Shayet wants to get at, not you or the Mir's men. Don't forget that. And he won't let Bianca go free until he has his hands on just what he wants." He spoke with such bitterness that it surprised me.

"And that being?" Toby shot at him. For no reason at all, his words sent a prickle of fear over my whole being, and I shivered, leaning closer to the fire, and waited for that answer.

But David was not so free with his secrets. He shifted his long lean body; then, after a brief silence, he looked at me and said quite unexpectedly:

"Miss Butler. Are you willing to be a part of this plan?" He stared at me, holding my gaze unwaveringly.

I expected a burst of disapproval from Toby, but it did not come. "Yes, of course," I said without hesitation.

"Very well. Now we may just have a plan that could be successful, Roberts. But it is all based on complete surprise, which the Kirghiz won't suspect until it's too late."

"Let's hear it, then," Toby said, sitting back, his eyes narrowed through the smoke haze.

"I will take Miss Butler with me into Khan Shayet's camp. It won't be as dangerous as it sounds, and they won't be expecting it. They won't have gone into their yurts as yet, but will be out in the open ring. Bianca, of course, will be in the big yurt with the women, Khan Shayet's women, for they retire long before the men do.

"By taking you with me, Miss Butler, that will throw them into confusion, and I can almost guarantee that you will be taken immediately to that yurt where she is. Your part will be to rouse her, find out if she is bound or not. Most likely, she will be in the rear of the tent, farthest from the door.

"But remember this: those women will be guarding her, for they will consider her their enemy. They don't comprehend English, but they are clever enough to understand actions. So do a lot of talking, but without your hands. Less action until the ripe moment when Robert comes. Be warned though, of those women. They can fight like wild animals.

"Roberts, Khan Shayet will want to deal with me, and you must take your position behind the big yurt as quickly as possible when we leave you. One of the men can give you the signal. Then, you make your move swiftly and don't waste a second. That is all you'll have, just seconds, to get her out of that yurt —and don't wait, not for anything out there in the ring of trees. Once the alarm is out, the whole horde will be clamoring for blood."

We were all silent, for David had finished speaking. Approval of the plan was written on Toby's face, but he said nothing, and continued to puff on his pipe. I spoke what was on my mind. "And how will you escape, David?"

His eyes squinted, but he didn't flinch. "Don't you worry about that, Miss Butler. I plan to distract the Kirghiz and his men with the only weapon I know. Trust me. Just see that Bianca gets out of there."

It didn't convince me, and I looked at Toby. He crossed his arms and said thoughtfully, "Well, it seems a sound enough plan, Markus. It's all we have, in any case. I'm all for it."

"Then we ought not wait much longer. They know we're here, but what they can't know is our plan. And we've got the snow for cover. Roberts, when you've got Bianca, get the hell out of there, and once back here, start back through the pass.

Tomorrow will be too late. Every second from this minute on counts. Don't forget it."

He stood up then, and without another word, he strode from the room. I was almost stunned by the valor the man was capable of. He was sacrificing his own safety for that of all of us! But what else could he do?

Toby too stood up, placing his pipe back inside his pocket after knocking the burned tobacco out into the fire pit. He spoke to Jaseen and Gulam. "Be ready when we return. We shall take three men with us, and two will stay behind to have those animals ready. Jaseen. You and Gulam make certain the packs are safe. We should be back well before dawn. Be waiting."

I saw the excitement leap in Jaseen's eyes. He and Gulam readily agreed. Then Toby turned to me, as the two men began to scramble together all of our gear.

"Here is a weapon you must have, Tawny. Put it down inside your boot and, for your sake, use it if you have to."

He brought out a dagger, hardly five inches in length, but out of its sheath, the blade gleamed deadly in the firelight. "You aren't afraid, are you?" He suddenly covered my hand with his. "You must use it. Don't hesitate." He ordered, but I heard the tender note in his voice.

I shook my head firmly, even as I shuddered with revulsion of what lay behind that order. But I was determined to go through with it, and I would use the dagger if I had to. I lifted my skirts and slipped the slender weapon, sheathed, down inside the fur-lined boot even as he watched me.

We were ready. It would take us an hour to get to the camp, circling it through the densely set trees which grew thickly along the Panj, and, estimating an hour to return, Toby was adamant when he spoke to the tall, broad-faced Hunzukut warriors who were to be left in charge of the yaks; they must be saddled and ready for instant flight. Those men smiled and nodded, for Markus had already outlined our plan to them, and to the three who would be going with us.

We started out then, and the snow blurred our vision as we

left our camp behind. That hour did not seem long as we walked single file. We dared not take animals, for they would give away our presence too soon. As it was, when we neared the huge Kirghiz camp, which was on a slight rise away from the trees, we knew that we had acted upon the opportune moment.

It was there that Markus left us, taking one of the Hunzukuts with him. He was back in less than ten minutes.

"I was right. The men are in the ring outside the yurts. The big one, Khan Shayet's yurt, is set apart from the other smaller ones. It should be easy to come up from behind. One last-minute reminder, Miss Butler. When you do get inside the yurt, call Bianca's name, then move quickly to the back of the tent. You must warn her. And remember what I said about the women."

I nodded my head. Toby stood beside me and I felt his hand on my arm, encouragingly. "And don't forget what I said, my dear girl. Use that knife. Take care." I stared up into his face, the snow thick already on his dark beard, and I had mixed emotions. But I was too excited to know a real fear in that parting.

I smiled. "I'll take care, Toby. Rest easy." And then I turned and found Markus's hand on my arm, guiding me through the trees, with one of the Hunzukuts behind us, while Toby and the two others would follow in five minutes. We walked some yards away into the thin outer edge of the trees, and then, giving a signal to the man behind us to stop, David led me a few feet farther along, just to where the yurts rose in deep shadows in the curtained snow. Then he stopped and turned to face me, very close. "Miss Butler," he whispered. "I want your promise of something."

"Of course," I said recklessly. "What is it?"

"If something should go badly wrong, I want you to take Bianca to her brother. I must rely on your promise. I can see that you have what is considered common sense about you, and Bianca does not have such a virtue. She acts before she thinks, but then, she is such a child. She will need you. Take her to her brother."

I was filled with dread, and no little surprised. "You speak as if you don't intend to be with us," I said, my heart hammering so loudly that I could hardly hear myself speak.

But he was not listening to me, pulling something out of his inside breast pocket. "Take this. It will be safe with you. Give it to Lord Gordon when you see him. But know one thing, Miss Butler. I made Bianca my wife before all this began. The child is legitimate. Our marriage document is with this packet and—other valuables. Please see that they reach Lord Gordon Harding. I must have your promise to take her to that safety."

He thrust the packet into my hands, and I barely had time to stuff it down inside the long pocket made into the fur lining of my tunic. "But—of course I promise. Yet you will be with us, with her! You must!"

He smiled; even in the gray-white blackness of night, I saw that smile, and a terrible dread filled me.

"Trust no one else with that packet, Miss Butler, and don't be frightened. Remember this. Tobias Roberts is a sure bet on getting through in the very thick of things. Count on it. And, I will tell you something else, if it will relieve your mind. Your brother is not dead. But I don't know where he is. He was onto something real big. But we've no more time. Let's get on to playing this very real charade for the big Kirghiz chief. Everything is at stake. Good luck, Miss Butler."

We could see Toby and the men crouching as shadows behind us, but not even a small sound escaped anyone. Then David took hold of my arm with a fierce grip, and we began walking in fast strides away from the shelter of the trees and across the snow-frozen turf to the edge of the camp.

As we approached the open ring, I saw the big fire pit dug in the hard ground, over which hung a spit with a lump of charred ibex still sizzling, and with men eating great hunks of it. The snow fell, hitting on the flames, and blue-black smoke, acrid and tantalizing, curled up into the dark broad faces around it all.

It seemed to happen all at once. I glanced around me, and saw that we were surrounded by the bandoleered forms like a

wall closing in on us. "Don't be afraid," David whispered close
to my ear. "It's all right. I promise you." And again, his hand
made a pressure on my arm as if to reassure me of that statement.

Nothing in my past life could have prepared me for this moment, however: David Markus faced the big Kirghiz chieftain,
with me by his side. Those dark glittering eyes moved from
David's face to mine with a surprised expression on his face.
David had been right; the man was confused; it showed openly
for that brief moment. Never have I experienced a chill of uncertainty such as I did under the quick scrutiny of that man.

He was big and the title of the big Kirghiz seemed fitting.

He stood with his legs apart; they were wrapped in sheep-
skin, and strapped in leather. His fur-trimmed tunic gave him a
regal look, but his head was bald as that of a bronze god. With
a flick of his fingers, I was suddenly seized from behind. I
gasped in the sudden terror of it, but David turned and gave
me a swift look.

That look sobered me more than anything could have done
in that moment. The Kirghiz was not interested in me; it was
David Markus whom he wanted.

I couldn't have struggled had I wanted to, nor did I cry out,
as I was taken from that eerie scene. I'll always remember that
it was the last I ever saw of David Markus. I could have sworn
that he had planned it all the way it happened that night. And
I never saw such blatant fearlessness as he faced that big
Kirghiz chieftain that night. He was braver than any man I
knew.

I was taken to the large yurt and roughly thrust inside, and
the flaps of the tent were stretched down tightly again on the
outside by the guard, who carried a rifle and who would remain
there, I suspected.

Except for the burning yak dung in the center brazier, the interior was dark, just light enough for me to see the forms of
several women and children already bedded for the night.

"Bianca!" I cried out. "Where are you?"

A form sat up suddenly in the rear of the tent. "Tawny? Oh,

Tawny Butler! Is that really you?" And to my amazement, she stumbled up from the masses of fur rugs and ran to me, throwing herself into my arms. She was crying. "I didn't ever guess that you'd come, not this far!" Her voice broke on a low sob.

"Don't fret over what is done, Bianca," I said, my own voice catching. But I remembered what David warned me of, and hurried on. "We haven't much time. Take me back to your sleeping place. Quickly." I glanced around me and saw the curious faces of some of the women, who were now sitting up on their pallets of fur.

"They don't understand English, but they do understand actions and expressions, Tawny." I nodded, keeping my arms around her. I was glad of the darkness, for it hid much of our expressions.

"Tell me quickly. Are you all right? Have they—harmed you in any way?"

"No. The women have been rough, but I have my maid with me. For the most part, we're both left alone. Did—David—come with you?"

"Oh, yes. Toby and the Hunzukut men are about to rescue us. So be prepared. It could be any moment now. We must get back to the rear of the tent." She led me back to her pallet. It was a large tent; I glanced around and believed I saw animosity as well as distrust in those faces closest to us.

Bianca solved much of this distrust by insisting that I lie down with her in the pile of fur rugs she had been sleeping on. At first, I thought this was unwise, but then I realized it was to slip unnoticed into her own fur-lined tunic and boots, which she had removed when she first lay down, and to strap a long flat leather pouch to her waist beneath the tunic, unseen by those beautifully untamed eyes in the faces of a proud nomadic tribe of women.

It was all so unreal. We talked openly but in subdued voices, and then Bianca cried softly into my shoulder and told me of the events which had brought her into the hands of Khan Shayet.

Not a murmur came from any of the women and children,

and they seemed to accept what had happened as nothing unusual; they settled back down into their sleep, for I heard an occasional snore. We lay fully dressed under the furs, waiting, listening, talking.

Bianca told me that the woman next to us was a Hunzukut girl who had been taken with her. She said, "Her name is Chanda, and David wanted me to have her in any case. She came with us from Gilgit. She must go with us tonight, Tawny. I will not leave her behind."

I studied the dark eyes in the wide face, and I believed that I saw no little fear there. But I pressed her hand for encouragement, and then I knew she did understand that something was about to happen. I noticed too, that she was fully dressed. So, we waited.

"I'm pregnant, Tawny," Bianca whispered. "I'm frightened, but I—I know David would not have had all this happen, had he been able to escape Khan Shayet. You believe that, don't you? Whatever happens, please never hold this against David."

I heard her pleading his cause, and I kept seeing in my mind that brave young man facing that enemy of his. I wanted to cry too, for I remembered I hadn't had time to thank him for telling me of my brother.

"I never shall, Bianca. You can count on that," I said softly.

The minutes crawled by; I had no idea of the time that was passing, or of the drama that must be going on in full outside in that ring. It seemed hours since I'd left Toby and stood with David out there in the veil of snow. I strained my ears for any sound that would tell me Toby was near, but no sound like that came.

Had something gone wrong? Could those last words of David's have been prophetically now coming true, that something could go badly wrong? My heart thundered madly as I listened. I knew I had to stay awake and keep Bianca and Chanda alert too for what was to come.

The sudden and furious beat of drums filled the night outside the yurt, and with it bloodcurdling cries, and a thunderous sound of horses rushed into the camp. In the next frenzied second, all pandemonium broke loose; all the women in the yurt scrambled up from their pallets, and their wild screams at each other deafened any other sound that might have come. It was a fearful scene, as they began pulling their clothes on. It was a madhouse.

Bianca and I stood up, the Hunzukut woman beside us, and we watched in horror as that front door flap was torn open and a blazing torch was flung inside; in that instant, I heard a familiar voice ring out behind us, "Tawny! For God's sake, get the woman and get the hell out of here!"

I turned, my heart plunged downward in one great thump. It was Gavin! He had sliced though the goatskin yurt side. "We've a God-given split second in all this hell turned loose!" He shouted, but no one in that flame-lit tent heard him or cared as I gave Bianca and her maid a push through the opening, and stepped free myself.

Snow was driving sheets around the camp, and those murderous yells were coming from men on horseback, waving great curved swords in the air; it was a nightmare beyond belief. Between the yurts, in one split second in all that havoc, I saw a man on horseback lean over a running woman who had run wildly from the yurt, and he swooped her up to him by her long black hair. She screamed as he pulled her onto his saddle, his war-cry age-old, like some demon let loose from inside him.

We ran across the frozen ground, and I noticed Toby was not with Gavin even as we ran down the slope to the edge of the trees. By that time, the snow hid the horrible scene, so garishly unreal behind us.

"It's a raiding party of a rival tribe, totally unexpected, but by God, how timely!" Gavin said close to my ear. "But we've no time to spare. Hurry on! Follow the guide." He grabbed Bianca's arm, and one of the men took hold of Chanda's. But I screamed out, "Gavin! Where's Toby?" as I ran ahead after our guide.

"Don't worry. He's with—helping Markus! Hurry, Tawny! Don't waste one precious second!"

How we made it back to our shelter, where Jaseen and

Gulam were waiting with the two other men and the yaks, I simply don't remember. The night had thickened with the snow, and we piled into those lambskin saddles; single file, with each yak roped to the other, we struck out for the hills. I held out for the hope that Toby was coming along with Markus, and would reach us before we were lost to them. What I didn't know until several hours later was that one of the Hunzukut men had gone back for them.

I did not know when they caught up with us, for it was a blind time, trusting only the surefooted yaks and the guides. I suppose it was near dawn when our guides stopped us for a rest, making hot tea with such skill in all that driving snow that I had to marvel. We fell off our saddles too exhausted to speak, and I saw that Bianca and her maid were content to sink into their fur rugs, huddled together, and, I supposed, sleep.

But I searched around to see Gavin; I didn't see him, but to my delight, I saw Toby. "Toby! I—I was given a shock back there, you know!" I couldn't keep the gladness from my voice.

He placed his arm around my shoulders, and I felt his snowy beard against my cheek for a moment. Then he held me off. "Gavin's gone back there," he said. And I heard the grim tone in his voice, and he talked in a low voice. "Markus won't be coming. It's all over for him." He didn't change his tone as he said quickly, "He was brutally murdered, just before those drums began and the raid surprised them all. It was an atrocious act." He gripped my arms, holding me close enough so that I could see his face clearly.

"Khan Shayet was goaded into what he did, and deliberately, by Markus. I witnessed it all, and I have to admit it was and is an enigma in itself. What a fool he was to act so blatant, standing up to that Kirghiz, and antagonizing him, knowing he would pay dearly! Brave as hell, and he paid with his life for it."

I was stunned, and I felt the tears sting my eyelids somewhere in the blinding, stinging cold of the snow.

"But just as that happened, and the drums beating, the raiding party descended on the camp. And, by God, Tawny, if I didn't know better, I would have said that tribe might have been trying to save poor Markus. In fact, I'm almost sure of this, for your brother was the instigator of it all, no doubt about it, but perhaps there were scores to be settled between those two tribes. There's much I don't know.

"It does seem that an exact payment was made there somewhere. We can't waste time, though. For Khan Shayet didn't get what he was after, and he believes it will be with us. We've got to make it over the pass, regardless. Our lives depend on it."

I remembered David's smile, his words, and the packet he'd given me. My heart was wrung with sudden sorrow for him. He'd been the one who'd told me the news that my brother was not dead. "Where is Gavin, Toby? I was stunned when—when David told me that he knew Gavin wasn't dead, but that he didn't really know where he was! And how strange that it should be Gavin tonight, of all people! I must know why he was there, so—" Toby put a warning finger on my lips.

"We'll know in good time, my dear girl. Gavin has gone back to cover our trail, I believe. And don't worry if he does not follow. There's much I don't know but would give a lot to know. Who is the woman with Lady Bianca?"

"She's Bianca's maid. A Hunzukut woman."

"Providence, I'd say. She will need her."

I suddenly remembered Bianca. "Oh. She—she can't know about David," I said thickly. "She won't even suspect—" I couldn't finish, for my throat was tight.

"It's just as well. She can be told later. If you like, I will tell her."

"I'd like to be with you when you do," I said, trying not to show the deep feelings I had about David Markus.

"Tawny. Did Markus speak to you before you went into that camp? I must say I am puzzled. Did he say anything at all to you?"

"Yes. He told me that he and Bianca are married. And, he asked me if I would take her to her brother. He made me promise that, as if he knew what would take place. I'm sure of that now."

"And is that all he said?"

"He—he told me about Gavin—" I was about to say that he had also given me the packet containing the marriage documents and other valuables, but Jaseen brought us our bowls of yak-butter tea, and we gave ourselves to this moment. I glanced back to see that one of the men was rousing Bianca and Chanda for their tea.

I stirred myself to go to Bianca, but Toby held me back and we sank down on the rug, in the shelter beside one of the shaggy yaks, protecting us from the snow, and drank our tea slowly, saying nothing more.

The snow storm did not cease, but quickened in its fury down through the pass, and we were caught in its thickening belt. It was treacherous every step. Our guides were methodically struggling to keep the yaks on the trail, and I never even guessed how close we came to going over the precipices, for they were hidden by the curtain of snow.

I didn't know when day came or when night fell and ended; indeed, I couldn't even say how many days and nights that we were on that trail. It seemed to go on and on, and no one complained that we were frozen, exhausted and even faint from the high altitude, our faces blackened by the stinging snow.

It was somewhere in all this thickness that Toby learned of the pursuing tribesmen behind us. They were closing in, he whispered in my ear, and although I was fearful, I was also numb to feelings.

It was dark like nighttime when, hours later, our small party stumbled blindly into a sheltered courtyard where a lamp was glowing, hung above a thick timbered doorway. We were helped down off our saddles, and taken inside a room lit only by the fire pit. But even as I gratefully sank into a numbed black oblivion, I realized that Toby was not with us.

Just how long he and Gulam, along with the Hunzukut warriors, had been gone, I could not know, but Toby had disappeared back on that trail.

7

Days and weeks passed into months. Bianca suffered severely from the effects of that dramatic flight. It was many weeks afterward that I knew she had pneumonia, and I feared for her life. Grief was with me during those anxious days; it hung about my heart and my mind like some great bird hovering over me.

But time went on in that little home just outside a village in the foothills of northernmost Hunza as though the world outside it had ceased to exist.

The farmer and his wife welcomed us. Because Chanda was with us, she could tell them of our plight, and they understood that our men had somehow suffered the same fate at the hands of the warring tribesmen as her own young husband. I learned that Chanda, too, was pregnant, but she began to look after Bianca with a peculiar attachment I thought was beautiful.

The farmer and his wife had three young children. Nazar Shah's home was built of mud and stone, sheltered in a walled-in courtyard, one room upstairs and one down. We used the downstairs room because it was warmer in the winter snows. It had one window, and with the fire in the hearth in the center of the room, it was cozy enough.

I soon learned that Nazar tilled two acres of land around his house; barley and potatoes were his main crops, but he had a smaller amount of millet and wheat and gram. In the spring, he had carrots and turnips and greens, and his trees yielded apricots, pears and apples and walnuts.

Eight sheep provided milk for his family and wool for their homespun garments. It was around the new year that two sheep were slaughtered for meat. I was glad for this, as the staple diet of walnuts and apricots became quite boring.

Nazar showed me his rock shelter for the sheep outside the house, and two snug storerooms attached to the side of the house. The storerooms held great piles of dried apricots, wicker baskets filled with almonds and walnuts, and great jars of grain. From the ceiling hung strings of pears; they were wrinkled, but they tasted as fresh as if they'd been picked that day.

Jaseen had made himself useful in the out-of-doors with Nazar; and after a time, I began to help Nazar's wife, Soni, prepare our simple meals. Meanwhile, I waited for Bianca to recover, and anxiously waited for some sign of Toby and Gavin. My own health had stood up well after those first few weeks of arriving. But Bianca lay on the piled quilts in a small alcove, incoherent with fever and illness. When finally Bianca opened her eyes to a dazed state of living, I knew she would recover and I found reason then to rejoice.

We became friends; she was like a younger sister to me, and I cherished her more than ever and beyond my imagination. The time came when she was well enough for me to tell her of David's death. She took it with great forbearance, and I was proud of her resilience in accepting what could not be changed. And even when I told her that I did not know what had become of Toby or Gavin, she tried to cheer me with hope to believe the best and not the worst.

The family was glad that Bianca would live. One day, Jaseen brought in a bouquet of wild pink primroses he'd found hidden under a boulder, which meant that spring was on the wing.

As she gained back her strength, the days went by quickly, and we talked of our families, of each other, and of our hopes. Each day, the baby she was carrying grew, and she talked of the baby. I listened, and as I did so, I remembered my own experience, so tragic and so far away now, and I believed that was what compelled me to confide in her my story.

She listened quietly, her eyes large and wide and almost purple in their blue depths. It was when I told her of Lindsey Ash, that she looked stunned and cried out, "Oh, Tawny! I know her, and I hate her! She was responsible, in a way, for Gordy's not wanting to have me with him in Nepal!"

I looked surprised, and was. "You know Lindsey Ash Pearson?"

"Yes. She is a widow, of course," she said with a quick little catch in her voice. "Your—Neil. But. She sort of moved in our lives in London in the past five years. I was young, I know, but I resented her influence over Gordy. She came to see my godmother, oh, about a year and a half ago, I think, and I heard her boasting about how she would get Gordy as her next husband. I think it was she who must have warned Gordy that I was going to meet up with David Markus. For he never ever before cared about who or whom I should meet or not. Yes. I am certain it must have been she!"

This news sobered me deeply. It lay heavy upon my heart.

Bianca's words were soft. "Fancy that, Tawny, dear. You are like the sister I always wished I could have, and now, we have shared a similar experience in life at the same age!" She impulsively reached up and kissed my cheek, and took my hand in her own.

But I was disturbed more than ever, and uneasiness crouched inside my heart as the days began to pass from winter into spring with the melting snows. The fingers of sunlight began to prise their way in everywhere, with motes of dust dancing like gold into the old comfortable room.

I began to help spin the wool with Soni and Chanda which they had worked on during the weeks combing it. I learned to weave the homespun cloth which the family wore, and I found a source of strength and peace as I kept my hands busy.

Chanda's own child was growing heavily inside her, and it was obvious that they would give birth about the same time.

On the first day of March, Bianca's little son was born. And as if that were not enough for Soni and me, with the help of Nazar and Jaseen, Chanda went through her difficult labor. Her little daughter lived only five hours. Naturally all of us mourned Chanda's loss.

During the following weeks, Jaseen brought the first disturbing news from the village. The rumors were out that the much feared Kirghiz chief, Khan Shayet, was looking for the white women.

I questioned Bianca. Yes. She knew what Khan Shayet was after. "Tawny. David gave me a very valuable and priceless object of Chinese jade. I have it in my possession now. It's in a long leather pouch I keep in my skirts. There are a few ivory pieces, but the Chinese jade is priceless, he said. He had the matching one with him. I can't think what he must have done with it, if Khan Shayet didn't take them off him—"

"He gave it to me," I said, and between us, we brought out the treasures and stared in awe at the pieces. Both jade objects were beautiful pagodas. "He said they were worth a king's ransom," Bianca said. And I was disturbed.

When I said nothing, Bianca said, "My grandfather, old Lord Howard, had somehow acquired an extraordinary collection of valuable carved ivory, but there were two small pagodas of jade, just like these. They are still in the family, but I believe David hoped to sell these to make a profit, to prove to Gordon that he would not be penniless when I presented my husband to him."

"Did you know where the pagodas came from?"

"Oh, no. I never bothered. They were such pretty objects. I believe Gordon must know about them."

She wasn't well yet from giving birth to little Mark. She lay in bed with a fever and her leg had swelled badly. Chanda, whose baby hadn't lived, was strong again, a mystery to life, and her milk was making baby Mark a round cherub of health. Bianca played with him on her bed for hours, and then she would tire and fall back exhausted. I knew I should be glad for the time when we could take her out into the sunlight.

We didn't speak of the pagodas again; but I knew she was alarmed about the news of Khan Shayet as the days passed.

Thus it was no great surprise to me when one day, after she'd been brooding darkly, her face pale, that she said to me, "Tawny. We must talk, and you must decide that you will do this I ask of you. No. Please don't think I am worrying for nothing. Listen. Please listen."

"I am listening, darling Bianca."

"I want you to take Mark and Chanda out of here. Take them, to Gordon in Nepal. Now. With no delay. For my son's sake, take him to Gordon. There's no time to wait. You can get through. Jaseen will guide you, and once you get to Baltit, the Mir will give you assistance. I am not well enough. I—must get well completely even to go outside of this house. But you are strong and I know you'll get to Srinagar, where Khan Shayet won't dare follow. Please, Tawny!"

It was natural that I should oppose her, and at first I would not even consider leaving Bianca behind, taking her child and its nurse over a mountain trail I knew already was dangerous. I kept hoping that Toby and Gavin would appear, but as those days wore on, there was no news. I didn't know without a doubt if they were alive, or if they would have made it through that pass when the snows began to melt. There was no such luck, and I knew I was grieving for them.

But the rumors were growing, and it was from Nazar that we heard the latest. "You should go. Great bad chief come, he take. Time, go now. Our Mir will protect you."

And I understood that Nazar was even thinking of the safety of his own family from this bad bandit. But what of Bianca? "I just can't leave you here, unprotected, Bianca!" I cried.

"That's just it," she answered. "Go to Baltit, tell the Mir what has happened, and perhaps he will send for me—send some of his warriors to protect this dear family. And Soni will look after me until I am completely well enough to travel. Oh, Tawny! Please, you must take my son from this danger. I will give you the—pouch too, and you'll wear it under your skirts. Take them to Gordon, and tell him everything."

There was nothing else I could do in the end. I looked at the kind faces around me; I knew their world was hard to exist in, but everything was precious and dear, for it was their lives. I looked at Bianca, pale, lying in her bed as she had done since the birth of Mark, and I looked at him, a fat healthy baby who

THE JADE PAGODA 101

would survive because his wet nurse was feeding him. She, too, would survive on the trail. And with Jaseen to guide us to Baltit, we could have very little problems, I thought.

We made our plans carefully, and Nazar and Jaseen brought back horses from the village. Bianca and I talked of the day she would arrive in Srinagar. I knew that I should go there first, and perhaps I would be able to wait for her in my house. My intentions were to go to Baltit and convince the Mir that he should send for her, and she could be taken to the castle. Perhaps I could inform Lord Gordon of this peculiar situation, and he could take charge of it all.

Nevertheless, she gave me her leather pouch; I took it with great misgivings, hesitantly, for I was reluctant to carry so many valuables with me on my person. But I gave her my solemn promise I would give them to no one but her brother.

Her parting from her little son, Mark, was tender and heartrending to watch. "But you will be in Srinagar very soon, darling Bianca," I said, trying to cheer her. "You will take Mark to your brother. But until you do get to me, I will look after him. Chanda and I together will be a sure bet that he will grow into a sturdy laddie for his dear mother!" I laughed, trying to be lighthearted, but my laughter was hollow, because I wanted to cry instead.

She clung to me, then kissed Mark and gave him to Chanda.

I left my gift with Nazar Shah: ten gold sovereigns. They were stunned, for they had never seen such gold pieces in all their lives. But it was all I had to give for the care he and Soni had shared with us.

We left just before sunrise the following day.

*

No one could have predicted what went wrong with our plans; on the outskirts of Baltit, Jaseen learned from a passing caravan that the Mir of Hunza was not in his castle, but away on a hunting party; he also learned that Khan Shayet was this very moment camped in Baltit. We dared not go through, or even around the city, for that Kirghiz chief would know it.

Jaseen had another plan. "We go to Leh, down through Baltistan into Ladakh. Rich merchant has caravan going today. We hide as pilgrims going to the temples in Leh." Besides this, he knew his father would be there.

It was a roundabout way to get to Srinagar, but it seemed the safest and the only way we could go. The merchant welcomed us, and we joined his protective camel train down through the strange barren land known as Moonland, for it was where the moonstones were found.

The snow ranges of the Karakoram behind us all the way down were a great and long panorama of magnificent peaks which glistened white and pure, and when we neared Leh a full eight weeks later, that old capital of Ladakh kings was set like an oasis amid the ring of snowy mountains, with barley and wheat fields around it.

I can never forget the mystery and uniqueness of those lamaseries, those gompas we stayed in each night, built high on hills overlooking a panorama of rivers and fields, with ranges of the Himalayas all around. The Tibetans in their flowing woolen coats and embroidered boots fascinated me. This, then, was Little Tibet, as my brother had often told me that it was called.

Outside the town of Leh, the merchant pointed out the long *manis*, or what was known as prayer walls. They consisted of exquisitely carved rough stones bearing the inscription *Om mani padme hum*, translated, "O thou jewel in the lotus, amen." The stones had been set by pious monks who believed they possessed a magic power which brought peace to the soul after death.

We arrived in Leh. The merchant Gergen, who was going to Demchok and thence to Lhasa in Tibet on the morrow, bid us farewell, and Jaseen set about to look for his father.

After less than an hour away in the market, Jaseen returned to me and informed me that the caravans had come in, and that he'd seen the big Kirghiz.

We hid in Gergen's camel caravan going out of Leh; he didn't mind, but helped to disguise us well as pilgrims, and we traveled down the Indus to this border town, where we had to make another decision. Gergen had to stay awhile there, and we couldn't take the chance. It was he who gave us the best route into Nepal, and thus, with our surefooted yaks and pack ponies, we took our hurried but secret leave from our friend.

We were certain that Khan Shayet was following us; Jaseen kept insisting that we would find safety once we reached Nepal.

*

It was Chanda who woke me from my troubled sleep in the old gompa by shaking my shoulder gently. I opened my eyes to a room smoky with the curious gray light that comes before dawn. Then I realized I had somehow managed to sleep after all, and remembered that another long day was ahead of us.

It was customary to leave gifts of offering with the abbot, and I did not hesitate to leave a considerable amount this morning. They provided the yaks which we needed to get down the mountain to the Karnali River, and had given us some provisions.

One of the Tibetan monks went as our guide. It took us two full days, but as we left the gompa that morning, a deep blood-red sun rose in the eastern sky; a clean, almost pristine day was to be ours, instead of the snow I'd thought we'd surely have.

Two days later, we arrived in the village where the royal caravan of elephants was making ready to depart for the journey to Kathmandu. I was more than pleased to know that we would be accepted as part of the train, for there were members of the royal family of Nepal traversing the long corridor of the valley to the capital of this old kingdom of Nepal.

No matter how I told myself later when I had time to think about it, I know I was not prepared to face the situation on the following morning when I stepped from the tent which Chanda and I were given on the first day out on that journey east. The sun was barely a crimson slice rising over the magnificent Annapurna range, but it was warm already. A man stood there, waiting for me.

The first thing I was aware of was his tallness; I am considered to be a fairly tall woman, but this man towered over me, dressed in neat khaki, the pants tucked into shining brown leather boots. The angry black eyes arrested me, but a moment later, I saw that they were not black at all, but a dark-hazel smoky color, stormy, and fringed with thick burnished stubby lashes, the color of his hair and closely cropped beard. He glared at me as if he wanted to strike me.

"Miss Butler, I believe?" His voice held no warmth, and even though the sun was warm in the semitropical morning, I felt the chill of that voice.

"Yes. I'm Miss Butler." I answered slowly, frowning up into those stormy eyes, and taking a step back from him as I let the flap of the tent fall into place.

"I heard that you had joined our party. At first, I couldn't believe it. You have a lot of explaining to do, Miss Butler." He was curt, rudely glowering down at me, his brows thickly meeting.

For no reason other than his odious manner, I lifted my chin defiantly and met that angry face. "Really, sir? What couldn't you believe? And just what have I to explain? I have not had the —misfortune to be introduced to you, so if you will excuse me—"

I turned to lift the flap to re-enter the tent, but he put out a hand on my arm to detain me.

"I beg your pardon, Miss Butler. Of course you don't know who I am. My name is Gordon Harding. I believe that you were given specific instructions in regard to my sister, Bianca Harding? I have just come from Srinagar, Kashmir, Miss Butler. I have no need to say how mystified I am by the complete silence of the past year. And now, to discover you are here— perhaps some light can be shed on the truth after all this time."

Had he struck me with his hands, I could not have been more unprepared. I stared, unable to believe the irony of the situation. A rush of dislike welled up like bitter gall inside me, but because I did indeed have much to say to him, I was defiant, even while my heart was hammering madly.

"Lord Harding. I am indeed—stunned to see you here, as well. You said you have been to Srinagar?" My eyes never left his. He nodded. "Was not your sister there?" But I somehow knew the dreaded answer.

"No, she was not there." His brows were lifted in speculation, I thought. "I would have thought you should have known that answer, Miss Butler."

It had been five months since I'd left Bianca in Nazar Shah's household; it was much longer than that since Toby and Gavin had rescued us from the Kirghiz chief, and when David Markus had lost his life. All my hopes, fervently believed in, had been that somehow my brother and Toby would have managed to get through any ordeal, but now I knew they were dead. Of Bianca, I had almost been certain that she would have made it down to Srinagar by the summer. I had nurtured that hope into actual belief, so therefore, my disappointment was a blow.

"Then, have you had no messages, Lord Harding?" My voice was thick with my fears. He had said there was complete silence of the past year.

"No, I have had no messages whatsoever, either from Tobias Roberts or from you, Miss Butler, not since he wrote to me to say that you had accepted my offer and that Bianca was there in Srinagar. And because of this silence, I went out there to learn just what was happening." He was impatient, darkly so.

"Then you can't have known what—"

"Gordon? Gordon! Have you seen that little wretch of a maid? I simply must do something about—" The voice and the woman materialized together in the soft heat of the morning, and she stopped and blinked, just as I stared almost open-mouthed to face Lindsey Ash Pearson.

Eight years had separated us and now, I suddenly recalled Bianca's version of how Lindsey Pearson had come into her brother's life, and her own dislike of this woman. I was bewildered by this strange quirk of fate that we were standing face to face again, and just as unprepared for it as I was to meet Lord Harding.

But whatever dislike I'd been prepared to feel toward him, that dislike was now one of contempt because of what I believed I saw between these two people.

I allowed her to speak first. She glanced at Lord Gordon. "Darling! How can this be? Tawny—Tawny Butler is standing here before my very eyes, and it is not my imagination!" She laughed, her red lips curving into a sardonic smile.

She had been standing a little way off, but she came forward, gracefully sure of herself, and I made it impossible for her to greet me with a kiss on the cheek or even to clasp my hand by stepping back and placing both my hands down into the pockets in my skirt.

"Hello, Lindsey," I said huskily, but indifferently.

"Tawny Butler! How on earth did you come to be here, of all places? Don't tell me that you connived an invitation from Her Royal Highness, Queen Lakhshmi Devi herself, to join this magnificent caravan of elephants to Kathmandu with us? And where on earth did you come from?" She stepped back, laughing, her eyes going over my person critically, and then she looked up at the man beside her, as if he would convince her of just how I came out of the bush.

There had been a time when I had believed that Lindsey Ash was the most elegant and sophisticated woman I'd ever known, and the most exquisitely groomed. On this particular morning, I wondered how she had managed to achieve a bandbox look, even here in the wilds of western Nepal. She wore the latest fashion in riding habits, made from a fine cloth of khaki, the skirt a little short over the polished leather boots. Her jacket fitted her slender form to perfection, and beneath the jacket, the shirt of tan cotton was tailored neatly. She was very attractive still, but I distrusted her.

"I am afraid it was not Her Royal Highness's invitation, but that of her steward, who managed to get me an elephant to Kathmandu, Lindsey." My voice was cool and distant. "I am fortunate, it seems." I glanced at Lord Harding's face. His expression was inscrutable, though he was scowling darkly.

"But how on earth *did* you get here? From where?" She gestured with her hand, bewilderment in her manner. She looked again at Lord Harding. "Darling? Did you know about all this? And you kept it from me?" She pouted with a coy look in her eyes, genuinely perplexed and gazed around at the colorful tented camp, now being dismantled for the move as servants and porters began taking down the tents to pack on the elephants.

In that brief speech, I thought I saw it all too clearly; it was the familiar tone of someone with shared intimacy. So that was the way it was, I told myself, hating myself for the little whisper of disappointment that seemed to touch my heart, even though I was sure I detected a small discomfiture in Lord Harding's manner.

"Of course I didn't know Miss Butler was here," he said smoothly. "But now, I suggest that you get on with your packing. I must speak with Miss Butler, and it is important. We haven't much time, and you have many things to attend to." It was a dismissal, and she didn't like it.

"Surely what dear Tawny has to say, Gordon, darling, should be my interest too. We are the very best of acquaintances, are we not, Tawny, dear? My maid is hired to do that packing."

"Nevertheless, I insist that I speak with Miss Butler alone." He was adamant, and he stepped aside, waiting for her to leave us, his hands clasped behind him. His arms were brown from the tropical sun, I noticed, in the short-sleeved shirt, as well as his long slender hands when he unclasped them.

Lindsey could do little else but to leave, yet she looked at me as she turned to go. "Tawny, dear. We must have a little chat too. Don't forget it." She smiled, and it rankled me more than I had wanted it to that she could get under my skin again so easily. But she smiled at Lord Harding. "Come to me when you've spoken to her, darling. I'll be waiting." He only inclined his head to one side as she left. We both watched her walk away to disappear among the gaily striped tents that were somehow beginning to resemble giant mushrooms flattening out. I knew that there must be scores of attendants in this party, perhaps fifty or sixty and maybe more, traveling eastward.

I turned to find him scrutinizing me, and under such a look, I felt a hot tide of embarrassment rush to my cheeks. He was comparing me with the well-groomed Lindsey; my clean but simple homespun cotton skirt and shirtwaist had seen wear and tear, and was faded. The sleeves rolled up to my elbows, and my arms were tanned, as indeed my face and neck were, not at all ladylike. I had discarded my long tunic and felt already the sweltering heat of the tropical valley after having known the cold clean mountain air!

It was only then that I realized I had not pinned my hair up in its usual knot; it hung down like a long hot cloak over my shoulders. I was uncomfortable to say the least. I heard Chanda moving around inside, and I saw Jaseen appear from around the tent to take my instructions, but I gave him a signal to wait.

Lord Harding caught that signal and turned to look. "Is that your servant? Pray do, have him to see about your packing."

"This shouldn't take but a moment, Lord Harding," I said coldly, trying to be as remote from feeling as I could. "What I have to say to you—"

"Miss Butler," he interrupted just as coldly, "I will not waste time in arguing. You have much to say to me, and I insist that your servant take care of his duties while we take a walk and you can explain everything. We have, I should think, two hours at the most before Her Majesty and the Prime Minister are ready to move for the day."

I was annoyed, and in my hesitation, he assumed authority and spoke to Jaseen. "Please carry on with whatever packing duties you have. Miss Butler and I have some business to discuss. We shall return shortly."

To my dismay, Jaseen smiled knowingly, touching his forehead in the manner that his old grandfather had done in assent, as Lord Harding took my arm and began to lead me away through the maze of tents. His hand was hard on my flesh, and his long strides left me practically running alongside of him.

We headed toward the riverbank, away from the camp and the village beyond, and away from the huge gray beasts that were to carry their burdens hundreds of miles through the lush valley eastward. Only when we were out of earshot of anyone did he slow down, but he locked his hand firmly on my arm and said harshly, "Let us stroll along this path now while you talk. I warn you, Miss Butler. Leave nothing out."

I tried to pull free of his grip, but he did not let go. "I prefer to walk as we talk, Miss Butler. I can assure you, I shan't let you out of my sight until I know all the facts. Where is Tobias Roberts? And where is my sister?"

Never had I been so indignant! I knew he would have all the answers, and I would be the one to tell him. Yet I was never so angry in my life at his arrogant behavior. Here was a man who would bully anyone to have his own way. I despised him with my whole being in that moment.

"Lord Harding! Let go of my arm this instant, or I shan't say one word! Of all the impossible, odiously mannered men I have met, you, sir, have no comparison!"

He turned, not taking his hand from me, stunned, I thought, that anyone could have spoken to him so. He glowered darkly, his anger meeting mine, and for a second I thought he was going to shake me. To my astonishment, he suddenly took his hand from my arm and stood back.

I gritted my teeth to keep from slapping his face, and began rubbing my arm, where I knew I should have a bruise. The man was an impossible rogue!

"Now, if you please, Miss Butler." I had the distinct impression that he distrusted me.

The sun struck warmly on our faces in that moment, and in spite of my own distrust of him, as well as being indignant, I knew all my anger had fled. "There is no reason for you to be so stirred up, Lord Harding," I said quietly, knowing I had full composure. "I was on my way to you in Kathmandu."

This took him by surprise. But I said, "Are you sure that you did not receive the message Toby sent to you from Gilgit? Last September, I believe."

He stared at me oddly. "No. I received nothing. That is why I am deeply puzzled. Toby was usually explicit with his intentions."

"I do not know where Toby is, Lord Harding." I told him everything; the words tumbled out. I kept nothing back. He listened, saying nothing, never interrupting through the whole thing.

There was no reason to leave anything out. "The winter passed somehow, and Bianca's little son was born—" I heard an intake of breath, sharp, and Lord Gordon swung me around to face him, for I had turned away, painfully recalling all those weeks of waiting, of knowing Bianca as a sweet adoring person. I didn't know until that moment that I had tears in my eyes, and they spilled over, wetting my cheeks, and I brushed them away with the back of my hand.

"My God!" he exclaimed, and I was vaguely aware of the shock in his voice. Even in the sunlight, I saw his face blanch under the deeply tanned skin. "What are you saying, Miss Butler? That Bianca had a child?"

With quiet dignity, I met his eyes and said proudly, "Yes. Bianca had a beautifully healthy little son. David Markus's son." I did not waver, and when he was silent to this, I went on. "That is why I am here, Lord Harding. I have brought Bianca's son to you."

For a moment, I thought I saw something almost human beneath that hard surface, something like a fear. "Miss Butler? Are you telling me my sister is dead? But you asked me earlier—"

I lifted my hands in a gesture to reassure him this was not so. "She was very ill after we arrived in the Hunzukut farmhouse, Lord Harding. But she recovered, and her health came back slowly. Having her baby simply weakened her again. But she could not make the journey. She begged me to take her son to you."

And then I told him of the Kirghiz chief, Khan Shayet, and

of the reasons why I fled from him down into Leh, through Ladakh, and of the pursuit.

"And the child? You have him with you here in this camp?"

I nodded, inclining my head to one side. "He is a very healthy strong child. Chanda looks after him well."

He was astonished. "You are an amazing young woman, Miss Butler. You have done a most incredible feat, journeying down through the most rugged part of the Himalayas. I—humbly—apologize for my—depraved conduct earlier. I beg your forgiveness. You have suffered much, it seems."

This took me by surprise. He reached out and took my hands in his, suddenly, warmly, and I saw a gentleness I was certain he kept veiled too often in those stormy gray eyes. He brought both my hands up to his lips and kissed them. "I feel most humbled by what you have done."

I felt a deep blush of embarrassment, but I was moved deeply, and I knew I wanted to weep, so I pulled my hands free and turned away. We heard the clear bells ringing in the morning light, bells for the Rani's prayers to be offered to Vishnu, around a Hindu shrine that was built beside the river. They sounded pure and clean as the air itself was, and I turned to look back. We had walked quite a distance from the camp, but even here, I could see the larger and more elaborate tents of the Rani were still intact.

We stood in a cool shady green glen on the riverbank. The sinuous, almost silken green torrents of the river rolled past us swiftly, and I shivered with a sudden apprehension, for I could not help remembering that last burning bridge high over this same Karnali River only a few days before.

We had escaped miraculously; little Mark was safe now. I could leave him in the care of Lord Gordon, and hand over to him those valuables which had caused so much fear and death already. And if Khan Shayet followed me here, then Lord Harding could deal with him. My duties were fulfilled.

I turned back to face Lord Harding, and found him watching me. "I would like to find Bianca, Lord Harding. I would like to know that she is safe. The Mir of Hunza, I know, would have offered her sanctuary, but had she been able to get there, then I'm certain there would have been a message for you in Srinagar."

He moved closer to me. "Miss Butler. Your concern for my sister is touching. I promise you this, that I shall leave no stones unturned until I do discover where she is. Will you trust me?"

8

There was a shout, and we both turned to see a servant running toward us, his red jacket brightly worn over the white baggy pants, and his brown bare feet leaping over the stony path with skill. Behind him stood the dignified form of some official with two young Gurkha soldiers with rifles on their backs.

The servant came closer, then stopped at a proper distance, and then bowed deeply. "His Excellency want to speak you. He say, please forgive, but come."

Everything closed up on Lord Gordon's face. He was immediately all protocol and more; he was in his trained profession of the diplomat, second only to the British resident himself, Sir Henry Lawrence, to whom Lord Gordon answered.

"Very well," he said crisply. "Go back to His Excellency and say I will come." The servant bowed again, while his crafty gaze lifted and touched my face briefly. "Yes." And he ran back downstream toward the waiting Prime Minister.

Lord Gordon turned back to me. "I shall introduce you to the Prime Minister, Jung Bahadur Rana, in a few moments, Miss Butler. We shall have to continue our talk later. But now, I want to give you a small warning; you must be on your guard at all times during this leisure journey to Kathmandu. I won't go into detail at this short notice, but it is most imperative that you say nothing of where you have been, or why you have come, except to meet me."

It astonished me, and I could hardly see any reason for the warning, but he said, "I will make this clear to you in stages, Miss Butler, believe me. You see, we are surrounded by a royal intrigue of the utmost secrecy and scandal. More than this, spies are everywhere, and suspects are watched. You, being a lone Englishwoman, having just come down from God knows where, will draw much attention to the Rani.

"She has her lover with her, as well as the Prime Minister, and several members of her family. You will be asked to attend her, I'm sure. Thus I am asking that you say nothing of my sister, or Markus and your brother."

"All right," I said, frowning, and he took my arm and started walking with me slowly toward the waiting Prime Minister. "This has been a royal hunt, and they are now on the return. As you already know, I have been in Kashmir, and it is my duty to attend them back to Kathmandu in lieu of Sir Henry. I joined the caravan in Rekcha three days ago. Lady Lindsey joined us there too, for she had arrived from Delhi."

I was astounded. "*Lady*—Lindsey, did you say?" I glanced up at him, quite puzzled.

"Yes. Lady Lindsey Pearson. I believe you were close friends at one time? But, Miss Butler, I am informing you of all this so that we won't have conflicting stories when the questions are asked. I learned of your presence in the caravan from the Queen's steward only late last night. But I waited until this morning to talk with you. Will you allow me to ask this one favor from you, Miss Butler?"

Surprised, I merely inclined my head that he could ask.

He laughed. "I dare say, but you will think it an odd one. However, I should appreciate it if you will say that the baby, Bianca's child, is yours. No harm will be done, and he will be safe enough. It is for security reasons. Bianca's estate is vast, and there are some people in this very train who know this. Please. Do I make myself clear?"

He was looking at me, and I was suddenly apprehensive. "Are you saying that Mark is not safe, if he is known as—her—heir?" It came to me that Bianca could be dead in that moment, and it took my breath away with alarm, like a quiver through my heart.

"Precisely, Miss Butler. I fear that will be our greatest care now. Have I your consent then, to let it be known that the child is yours?"

"Of course!" I cried. I was anxious to hurry back to Chanda where Mark was.

He smiled. "Please don't distress yourself, Miss Butler. I shall be close and in touch every hour during this journey. But just remember that you have come here to meet me, and nothing more."

By this time, we reached the Prime Minister of Nepal, and if my color was high and my eyes blazing with some inner fire because of all this conspiring talk, the man who faced us did not seem to notice.

Though he was short in stature, Jung Bahadur Rana gave the appearance of being tall, for he bore himself with such dignity and pride which all the peoples of these Himalayan kingdoms possessed, and which I had observed throughout my contact with them.

Dressed impeccably in white, with a scarlet sash across his coat, this polite young man bowed stiffly to me when Lord Gordon introduced us. He then inquired after my state of comfort with the tour, and he had all the little graces of someone not quite interested in what I actually felt, but was practicing a requirement which he had cultivated with a cool charm.

I answered him politely, assuring him of my comfort, and then I withdrew with the excuse I had to hurry back to the camp, and I left them both watching me as I hurried past the two young Gurkha soldiers who stood at attention. I made my way back into the chaotic tent-packing to find that ours had not yet been taken down.

I rushed inside to see Chanda munching on freshly baked chapati, which Jaseen had procured from the cooks while I was gone. He had brought in fresh fruit too, and when Chanda saw me, she gestured to the plate of food she had set aside for me. I saw that she had carefully packed our things, and that Mark was already fed and lying down on the clean blanket.

"Thank you, Chanda," I said, suddenly dispirited for no reason at all. "I must do my hair first." And indeed, I was annoyed that I had not done it up properly first thing this morning.

"I do hair for you," Chanda said at once. She bade me sit down beside the baby and brought the plate of food and the pot of tea she had ready for me. While I ate, she had her fingers in the masses of my hair, brushing it with skill, then smoothly wound it into a heavy knot on the nape of my neck.

I glanced at Mark, who gurgled pleasantly beside me, holding in his tight little fingers the little seed rattle Jaseen had made for him. I tickled his toes and he laughed the sweet laugh of a contented healthy baby. I picked him up suddenly and placed him in my lap. He smelled scrubbed clean with soap and powder, and I looked down into his cherubic face.

He was beautiful, and I suddenly wished that he were mine. But even as that thought came, a great sadness wrung my heart, for I remembered that hour Bianca had parted from her son. I knew I would do anything to get him back into his mother's arms. For I would not believe that Bianca was dead. She had trusted me with her son's life to get him to the safety of her brother, and this I had done. But I had to hold on to my hope that she was still alive.

Lord Gordon wanted me to protect Mark now by saying that he was my own. I was willing, knowing it would cause me no grief. But I thought of Lord Gordon's warning words. Who could possibly be a threat to this beautiful child in this caravan? Who could know of Bianca? Of David Markus? Or indeed, for that matter, who could know of my brother, Gavin Butler?

I shivered suddenly, in spite of the heat inside the tent, and I knew all over again the dreaded fear of the threat with which Khan Shayet had overshadowed my whole spring and summer.

All at once, I wanted to be free of the burden of having in my possession the valuable treasures for which that Kirghiz chief had murdered David Markus, and possibly my brother and Toby. I felt strangled by this weight, and to pass it over to Lord Gordon would do much, I believed, in restoring my peace of mind. I felt that by not having it in my possession, could be a safety measure for Mark.

Even as I was thinking these thoughts, and had made up my mind to hand them over to Lord Gordon at the first opportunity, I heard him speaking to Jaseen outside the tent. I was about to place Mark down, when the flap opened and Lord Gordon spoke. "May I come in, Miss Butler?"

He did not wait for my answer, but entered, and stood there looking down at me with Mark on my lap. I believed those eyes took in everything; Chanda, the brush that she was stowing away into the pack, me and the baby. Without a word, he strode over to me, sat down suddenly and lifted the child into his arms.

I'm sure I shall never know just what he truly felt in that moment, but I did see the unexpected surprise and pleasure in his expression as Mark laughed, the baby hand grasping hold of the neat clipped beard of his uncle.

Our eyes met as he was holding Mark, and something happened inside me, as if a sleeping chord had been struck.

Whatever might have been said was not spoken then, for there was a commotion at the doorway, and the flap lifted and Lindsey stepped inside, and I had to blink at her audacity; not only at this, but at what I had just experienced.

Her wide candidly brown eyes went from Lord Gordon to me, and I guessed then that she had summed everything up. "What a touching scene! Tawny!" She moved across the space to where we sat, and in that moment Lord Gordon handed Mark back to me and stood up. I had the impression that he had been caught unawares, and seemed none too happy about it.

But Lindsey said, "But, Tawny! A—baby? I had no idea . . ." She stopped and I had a queer sinking feeling inside me.

Lord Gordon said, "Yes, Lindsey. He is quite a handsome little boy. I commend Miss Butler—Tawny—on producing such a regular healthy child." His voice was deep with huskiness.

"But this is most surprising, Gordon, darling! Tawny, you do the most surprising things. May I see him?" She stepped closer and would have taken him, but I stood up and gave him to Chanda, then turned to face Lindsey.

"I fear we are next. I hear the porters clamoring outside to take this tent down. Thank you, Lord Gordon, for looking after —my welfare."

"Oh, not at all, Miss Tawny. Come along, Lindsey. I'm sure she has many things to attend to." He made to go, but Lindsey looked at me.

"But, Tawny. Who is the father of your child? I had no idea— Oh there! It must have been that Tobias Roberts. Come now. Confess the truth."

A small nasty silence rung in that stifling tent. Then Lord Gordon's laugh, one full of mockery, matched Lindsey's insulting accusations. "How did you guess, my dear Lindsey? Tobias and Miss Tawny were secretly married, so none of this was yet to be known. What I find most unusual is how you could have known. But let us leave Miss Tawny now." He took hold of her arm and ushered her through the door, and I heard her laughter echoing back to me.

"That was indeed a surprise, darling," she said. "Yet it is not hard to guess about Tawny Butler, because I know her very well. Still. Married, and to Tobias Roberts! Is this what she came to confess to you? Oh! What now, darling?" I heard exasperation in her voice, just as the flap lifted, and he stuck his head inside.

"I forgot to say that you will be expected to join the royal table for dinner tonight, when we make camp. You will then be presented to Her Royal Highness, the Rani of Nepal. It's a royal command. Meanwhile, I shall see to everything, Miss Tawny." He left then.

*

It was complete chaos until the elephants were loaded with their royal burdens and the guests of the Rani and those who, like myself, had attached themselves to the caravan for safe travel through the valley to the capital city of Kathmandu.

Chanda and I rode with Mark atop one of those huge beasts

in an elaborately canopied square box, which was draped in yellow muslin to keep out the sun. In front of the box sat the uniformed, turbaned driver, guiding the elephant with all its bright livery in the royal colors, which every single one of the train of fifty great gray animals wore.

A small column of Gurkha soldiers marched ahead, and a single file of them on either side flanked the leisure train, as did many of the porters. Most of the servants had piled on the packs designated for their masters. I had seen Jaseen climb aboard the elephant which carried our packs. He had been given instructions from Lord Gordon which he carried out explicitly.

I had mixed emotions throughout that day. Reason told me that Lindsey and Lord Gordon were more than just friends; hadn't Bianca informed me that Lindsey had plans to marry her brother?

But what did puzzle me more than anything was Lord Gordon's wish to keep Mark's identity a secret even from Lindsey. He had, with deliberateness, fabricated a marriage between Toby and me, with Mark as our child. So he did not trust even her with the truth.

It was clear to me now that Lindsey believed she had her power over me, and I wondered what she had revealed to Lord Gordon of my past and her own. That she was a titled lady gave me much apprehension. It could only have been Lindsey who had given that recommendation to Lord Gordon—*the* Lady Pearson, and not Lady Gillian, Neil's mother, whom I had believed had placed aside her unforgiving heart and recommended my character to Lord Gordon. But for Lindsey to have that title, Lady Gillian would have to be dead.

These were my thoughts throughout that day's journey. There had been a brief lunch stop, and although I was apprehensively waiting for the inevitable visit I knew Lindsey would make to me, I did not see her during this stop. Nor did I see Lord Gordon, except from afar; I could never mistake that tall lean figure in the stiff khaki uniform striding beside the smaller form of the Prime Minister on the banks of the river in the heat of the siesta hour, before we continued the afternoon's travel.

We left the Karnali River and followed a smaller stream, and it was quite late before the caravan stopped again for the night. The pale sunset was left undisturbed to soak everything in its yellow light as the porters made ready the tents. Chanda carried water for our use, and while I scrubbed my skin and then pulled out my only decent gown of pale-lemon muslin, she fed Mark and then put him down to sleep.

I dressed with care, and Chanda brushed my hair and arranged it with skill into the smooth knot, and surprised me by tucking a cluster of pale-tangerine hibiscus around it. I added a few drops of lavender water to my temples to cool my skin, and then I was ready.

It was not yet dark, but in the growing dusk I heard the soft deep gongs of the ancient temple on the far bank of the river, calling the monks to prayer. Through the open flap of the tent, I saw the soft-pink tangerine moon rise full, climbing in the thickening velvet of night. I saw couples leave their tents and stroll hand in hand toward the waiting tents of the royal party, and I felt a twist of pain and some strange emotion around my heart that I did not want to admit even to myself.

My heart fluttered giddily, however, when I heard a footstep near the tent, heard Jaseen's low voice, and I turned to the doorway. But it was not Lord Gordon who crossed the threshold into the tent without announcement. It was Lindsey. She was attractively gowned in white silk, with a flamboyant dash of scarlet around her waist, and in the fading light of the tent she seemed almost to glow.

"Tawny. I just had to come. We must have a little talk." She glanced suspiciously toward Chanda. "Have your maid leave. They have ears like elephants, and never forget what they hear, and always gossip."

"What you have to say to me, Lindsey, can be said here and now, with my maid in attendance. I'm sure we have no secrets —now?" My dislike of her was apparent even to Chanda, I was sure.

This made an astonishing impression on her face; even I could see how her eyes narrowed with her dislike of me, which was a great change in this woman who I'd discovered had never let her feelings or thoughts show. She had been quite devious in the past. It may have been my youth to have not known how to read such a person, but now she was not able to hide so much from me.

She shrugged her shoulders. "Oh, very well. Just as you please." She looked at Chanda, who had somehow ignored her and gone about putting things away, then settling down near the sleeping Mark.

"I must say, you do surprise me, Tawny Butler." She smiled lazily. "Gordon is displeased with me for giving such high recommendations on your character to look after his sister's affairs." She held up a hand when she saw my expression.

"It was something I felt I should do for your benefit, Tawny," she said gently, defensively. "Because of all that happened years ago. I wanted to somehow—make up for all that misunderstanding. Please believe that my best intentions were for your gain, not mine."

I could say nothing to this, for it didn't ring true. So I waited. She would make known her reason for wanting to talk with me. "What happened, Tawny?" she asked, frowning slightly. "I mean, to Bianca? Where is Gordon's fiery wild sister? I know that you must have been with her, you and Tobias Roberts. It was your lack of correspondence with Gordon that rankled him. He nearly went mad in the worry over that wayward child, and it was all I could do to keep him from going out to Kashmir before July! Your obvious power over Tobias, Gordon's right-hand man, left a blow where it hurts most."

When I didn't answer her outright, for I found this questioning quite absurd on her part, she showed a faint annoyance. I could see she was trying hard to win my confidence. She turned a full smile on me.

"Tawny, dear. Let's be friends. What's past, is over. I know you don't want to trust me again, but really, we can benefit much by joining forces, especially so now that you and Tobias are married. You see, Gordon and I—well. We are getting married very soon ourselves. It would be a load off my mind and my heart if you would find it in your heart to forget about the past."

I wanted to laugh, but even as I felt that scorn, I knew another feeling of despair, but I would not let her see that. "Tell me, Lindsey. When did you acquire her ladyship's title? I had no idea that Lady Gillian had died, or Sarah, for that matter. Surely Sir Lyle would have remarried? I don't remember that it was your place to even accept it, even if you were Neil's widow."

She was quiet to this, studying my face in the fast growing darkness within the tent. "So that's it; I see! You are puzzled over my title." She laughed. "Dear Tawny! I can read you clear through. Oh, yes. Lady Gillian passed from this earth, and Sir Lyle was only too happy to remarry, and I was available." She laughed.

"But now that I've confessed, you must also confess. Bianca is dead, isn't she? She ran away with that soldier of fortune, David Markus, didn't she? And she lost her life somewhere, possibly with him. Oh, I know all this. Gordon and I have been prepared for this truth, and now you have already told him. You must see that I should know about it too. Poor dear Gordon. He—loved that little naughty vixen, naturally. But she was a headache for him. She is—dead, isn't she, Tawny? You must tell me."

"You did not explain just why you are so free to marry Lord Gordon, Lindsey? Married to Sir Lyle, you would not be available surely?" I felt I saw just what she was doing, trying to pump me of information I had no intention of giving to her, and I was making her reveal her life's trail from the time I'd last seen her until now, knowing I was stalling for time.

"Poor Sir Lyle! He could not get over losing Neil. He was virtually a weak heart patient in the last months before his death."

My mouth was dry as if it had suddenly been stuffed with

cotton. "And so they never knew your deceit, in which you were going to take my child, to present to them as your own?" I knew that all the sting of my hurt pride was poured out in those words, with bitter contempt for all the injustice that had been wrought through this woman's diabolical, scheming mind.

A deadly silence hung thick between us. She lifted her chin with that old arrogance I remembered all too well, and even in the hot thick air of the tent, I could see just how much she had aged since that time. But I had grown too, and I faced her with a fierce pride, which unnerved her for the moment.

"I see," she said after that full moment of speculative silence. "So you have not forgiven, nor have you forgotten. Well, I did my best to help you out of a bad situation, so that your name and reputation would not be blackened. You were Neil's little . . . *doxy*. A son—his son would have inherited all that the Pearsons had to give him. As it all happens—well." She sighed deeply, almost regretfully.

"As it all happens, you were the one to inherit it all by marrying Neil's father," I said. "You find ways to get what you want, but not at my expense anymore. Now, if you will excuse me . . ." I walked over to the door, dismissing her.

She hesitated a brief second, a strange little smile curved on her mouth, and regarded me as if she were a cat toying with a mouse. "You are right, Tawny, dear. Remember it. I do get what I want." And she left me as though she had won a victory.

I was left with a vague feeling that Lindsey had made a veiled threat; but I shrugged it off, for what indeed could she threaten me with that would not involve her also?

But I kept asking myself, during the next minutes before I heard Lord Gordon speaking to Jaseen, why had she been insistent in wanting to know about Bianca? I distrusted her, it was true, because she had used me so when I was younger. Even in her attempt to make me believe that she was somehow apologizing for her own devious reasons for what she had done to me, I knew that Lindsey could never humble herself to admit that she had caused my suffering. It was a fact lodged in my own heart and mind, that Lindsey had ulterior motives working for every gain she could get from life.

I went over to look down on Bianca's little son; he was sleeping, and Chanda sat quietly near him, her hands busy folding the nappies into neat squares. She had been watching me throughout the whole ordeal with Lindsey. Now, her gold round earrings tinkled as she moved her head slightly, looking up at me, and said,

"You go. I look after Mark. He with me." She put a hand to her breasts, and suddenly I knew I should have no fears for his safety with Chanda.

I smiled at her. "Yes. And I trust you, Chanda. Keep your eyes on him. We can't let his mother down now, can we?" And I leaned over and touched the baby's cheek with my fingertips.

"He outside now. You go?" Her eyes flashed in the semi-darkness.

"Yes. I go. Take care, Chanda." And I went through the doorway, bracing myself to face this man and Lindsey. For surely, I thought, she would not give him one extra minute to be in my company.

Thus I was surprised when I stepped into the soft warm night to see him standing there without Lindsey, and waiting for me, talking in low tones to Jaseen.

He smiled at me, taking a step nearer. "I felt I should escort you to Her Royal Highness's shindig, Miss Tawny. I see it as my duty to present you."

"And . . . Lady Lindsey? She is not with you?" I heard the sarcasm, but I was determined that he should not know my feelings. It seemed that I now had to play a new role, yet it did have its drawbacks.

He laughed. "She has already found her way to the tables. I understand that you were both acquaintances at sometime in your past lives," he said, as we fell into step and began threading our way through the pitched tents.

How much did he know of that past? I wondered, and found myself biting my underlip. "She has told you of this, then?"

"Not much. But, let us not dwell on it, Miss Tawny. To-night, I shall present you to the Rani even as I did to the Prime Minister this morning, as Miss Butler. Strictly for reasons of consistency." He laughed. "And you can be guaranteed of the secrecy of your *marriage* to Tobias taking the caravan by storm. It all works out like clockwork. You . . . didn't mind, did you? I mean about my telling Lady Lindsey this?"

"Just as long as I know it is for Mark's concern, no. I didn't mind at all." And I remembered dear Toby and thought of what might have been had he not disappeared. I believed that he would have wanted it to be so. And now? What was my heart telling me? The man's warm fingers on my arm made my blood tingle, his nearness intoxicating, like the warm scented night around us. The stars lit up the velvet sky, and the moon was a glowing globe hung there for pleasure.

"Then we understand each other in this. I shall also introduce you to the other English members of this party tonight. Lady Jennifer Lawrence, wife of Sir Henry, the resident in Kathmandu, is traveling with their daughter, who arrived in India two months ago. They came up from Delhi with Lady Lindsey. The young woman has suffered from the heat of the plains, and she seems a bit under. The gentleman who will be joining the English party is a young employee of the East India Company, Sir Ralph Hodgson, who resides at the residency in Kathmandu, a sort of right-hand man for Sir Henry. But you shall meet them. The three ladies share a tent, which I'm told is beginning to be a trifle crowded."

I believed he was amused as he spoke, and indeed, I wondered just why he bothered to inform me that Lindsey was sharing her tent with the Lawrence family. Yet for an instant I knew a sudden little thrill of unexpected joy leap somewhere inside my heart. He was looking down into my eyes, and it seemed an eternity, that look; I was deeply aroused, and I knew it, but I wanted to deny it.

We arrived at the great canopied open tent, where a dais had been improvised to resemble a throne, which faced a fairly large audience room, around which low tables had been arranged, with bright-colored cushions on which the guests sat in leisure in the Eastern fashion.

Great glowing paper lanterns hung like silk glowworms from the center and around the sides of the canopy. Carpets covered the ground, and flowers scented the air. It was magnificent, for the Queen and her retinue sat upon the dais, decked out in full regalia.

We were among the last guests to arrive, and a servant led us to our cushioned places near the dais. And then Lord Gordon did a most unusual thing; the two empty places were at opposite ends, and in between were the three ladies and the English gentleman; Lindsey had obviously reserved the seat next to her for Lord Gordon; the remaining seat was next to the gentleman, where I would be seated.

Lord Gordon whispered into his ear, whereupon the young, almost pink-faced man with a bushy blond mustache nodded affably enough, rose from his place and took the cushion next to Lindsey. Lord Gordon then led me to the cushion next to the cream-faced woman and sat down next to me. I didn't even glance over at Lindsey; I simply intended to enjoy myself during this unexpected hour.

Lord Gordon introduced me to Lady Jennifer Lawrence. "I feel I already know you, Miss Tawny. May I call you Tawny?"

"Please do, Lady Jennifer," I said, smiling into a pair of refreshing periwinkle-blue eyes.

"I knew your brother, Gavin Butler—only slightly, mind you, but that was because he was seen so very little. However, Lady Lindsey has not spoken of anything else since she discovered that you were on the caravan with us. Tell me, my dear, have you been presented to Her Majesty as yet?" She lifted her fair eyebrows, smiling at me all too knowingly.

"No, I have not yet—" I stopped, for Lord Gordon touched my arm, and said to her, "It has been suggested that I present

Miss Tawny to the Rani, Lady Jennifer. The Prime Minister would have it no other way."

"Oh. But this is a most unusual, but delightful, change from the usual affair, is it not, Lord Gordon?" She laughed softly, meaningfully, at him; then, as he agreed, she touched my arm with her hand. "Now, you must be friends with my daughter, Jane." And the young woman on her right was remarkably like her attractive mother, but so very young and her face a blushing pink.

We spoke briefly, but I could see that she was more interested in just what the young man Sir Ralph was saying to Lindsey. So that was the reason, I thought, for her blush.

It was during the course of the meal, sumptuous by all Eastern standards, that Lady Jennifer revealed all the scandal of the royal court. Lord Gordon affirmed it, even as she spoke in low tones, while the musicians played on their long-necked sitars and drums, and the servants brought course after course of food to place before us.

The Rani, one of the most exquisitely shaped women I'd ever seen, sat in a glittering splendor of rich brocades and silk in the center of the dais. She wore a gold satin short-sleeved mandarin gown beneath the sheer, paler-gold silk sari, adapted from the Indian fashion; it was a mixture of Chinese and Indian, I noticed, and this tiny golden-skinned beauty could not have worn it to more effect; her long thick black hair was parted in the center and pulled back tightly into a heavy knot in back, and the Eastern crown gold set with huge emeralds.

Beside her, on the left, sat the young Prime Minister, Jung Bahadur Rana, and as Lady Jennifer pointed out, "Oh, my dear, but he was responsible for the assassination of Mataber Singh, the Prime Minister who was close to the King. Since his death, the Rani has had full control of the country, for she and the King are virtual enemies. She has her lover here with her, see, there on the right? He is Guggun Singh, a member of a very noble family of Nepal. But she is also being 'wooed,' as we call it at the residency, by none other than Jung Bahadur, with the help of the British."

Lord Gordon cautioned her to silence at that moment, so I gave my full attention to the royal party and the meal. Lord Gordon whispered to me for my benefit, "The young woman seated next to Guggun Singh is the Rani's sister. The two families have been very closely related for centuries. The young man and younger woman on the Minister's left are the Rani's daughter and son. And all those guests across from us are members of that household, various friends and relations whom she keeps to her bosom."

"When—when was the last Prime Minister assassinated?" I whispered, for I seemed to recall the rumor that it had been the plot of the Queen to rid the King of his trusted Minister. But it was Lady Jennifer who spoke.

"A year ago last May, and it was quite hideous," Lady Jennifer said, "I can tell you, for Sir Henry was terribly angry that it had all been handled so carelessly. It was a time when we all held our breaths, I can tell you." It was obvious that she had been quite upset about it, and of course, I saw the whole thread of truth in her statement; the British had a hand in the movement of the government, as it had in Ladakh; so I wondered now, how it would all turn out.

I also saw that Lord Gordon was frowning deeply, and I felt him stiffen beside me. "I would caution you, Lady Jennifer. We are not . . . shall we say, alone. And I must say, your daughter is looking so much healthier tonight. Perhaps this climate has improved her condition?"

"Oh, I am happy to say that is true, Lord Gordon. How very kind of you to take notice. But just between you and me, I think we have a budding romance on our hands." She smiled with what could only be the hope for her daughter's happiness. She did not seem in the slightest offended that she had been called down for her outspoken thoughts on the vital government situation.

"I hear that Sir Ralph is keenly interested in nature too. He has brought in many specimens of birds and flowers from the back country. I suppose Miss Jane would find that too taxing to be romantic." He lifted his brow, rather sardonically, I thought, amused.

But that dear lady was matchless in her indefatigable character. "Oh, not so, my dear! I believe it would do her a world of good. It's taking an interest which changes everything."

"Of course."

I wasn't sure exactly, but it seemed to me that Lord Gordon was being a trifle sarcastic toward this lady, who in her pale-lilac silk and cream lace was obviously enjoying herself to the hilt in all affairs; those of her daughter, and of her husband, with the weight that he carried in the Government of Nepal, and I suspected, of anyone else who touched her life. I shuddered inwardly, with a strange little curious look into the future, and decided I should have to be extra careful that she did not enjoy herself at my expense.

When the dinner was over and the servants had removed all the dishes, tea was brought, and the dancers came out and began to perform for us. Lovely Indian girls with bare skin under the sheer silk began a sensuous weaving of their bodies to the strange twang of sitar and drums, suggestive to the imagination, and so beautifully graceful that I could not take my eyes from them.

After these dancers left, another young woman came out, and she was a Nepalese, clothed more fully, but with no less charm and grace with her small exquisite form and face. She was a true performer, and the dance she performed in front of the Rani and her family seemed to convey all the obedience and submission she could give to her empress.

"They say she was a former girl-child goddess Kumari, this lovely dancer," Lord Gordon explained in whispered closeness, as the dancer knelt in front of the Rani at the end. "In Kathmandu, there is a palace in Durbar Square where this one goddess is chosen as a child to rule until she reaches puberty. She is not allowed to have a normal girlhood, and she is seen occasionally from the balcony, during certain festivals."

"She is lovely," I whispered back to him, just as the Rani rose from her place and stood facing the dancer. She walked down, after a servant placed in her hands a lei made of scarlet blossoms, and put them over the head of the kneeling girl, touching her head as if to anoint her. A sigh went up through the guests, and the Rani bowed gracefully and returned to her place of honor.

Then the young dancer rose and bowed herself out of the presence, while the musicians played a stirring country tune.

My presentation to the Queen of Nepal was not outstanding, except that when I stood in front of her, bowing in the curtsy her title demanded, the Prime Minister leaned over and whispered something in her ear. It brought an unusual flush to my skin, for she looked at me then, and at Lord Gordon, and I believed I saw something like speculation in those mysterious dark eyes, so cleverly made up. She was a shrewd woman, and greedy for power.

For no reason at all, I mistrusted that speculative look, and I was disturbed more than ever when I returned to my table. Why had the Prime Minister singled me out to the Rani's attention? I felt I should ask that question of Lord Gordon, but I saw that I should have to wait, for when we returned to the tables, Lindsey had taken my place beside Lady Jennifer, and looked up at me with a peevish coy air.

"Oh, Tawny, dear? You won't mind, will you? I do want to talk to Gordon," and she flashed a smile at him. I took the end seat, because Sir Ralph had moved to sit beside Jane.

Sir Ralph, in the company of Lady Jennifer and Jane, walked with me back to the tents and bid me good-night. I caught a glimpse of Lord Gordon and Lindsey slipping away in the moonlight, and I felt a tight squeeze of pain around my heart, knowing that my own feelings toward Lord Gordon had undergone a complete change. I was annoyed by this admission.

It was when I was already undressing for the night that I remembered I had not turned over the valuable collections to Lord Gordon, and I felt a tremble of anxiety. He had not been too anxious to inquire after them, nor had I given him what papers David Markus had requested me to do. Thus, I was restless, and slept very little that night.

9

During the following ten days and nights of our travel eastward, the caravan routine was virtually the same pattern as that
first day and evening had been. The mad chaotic rush to pack
the tents and boxes on the elephants every morning; the travel
until midday for short lunch breaks and a siesta time, because
the sun was strong; then a full afternoon of travel with the sun
at our backs, and making camp at sunset. Then the utter confusion all over again amid the porters and servants pitching the
tents and lighting the fires for the cooking.

There was always the open canopied tent with tables and
cushions set up for the guests to partake of the evening meal,
but not always did the Rani appear. At those times, there was
very little gala entertainment, but nonetheless, the evenings
were exotic all on their own, and with the glowing paper lanterns to light our dinner hour, it seemed like magic.

If I had entertained any thoughts of Lord Gordon seeking
out my company during those strange lovely evenings when the
purple drifted down over the wild lush valley we traveled
through, I was sadly mistaken, for he did not do so. He and
Lindsey were together mostly during those romantic nights, for
I saw them walking away side by side, deep in conversation
after the dinner hour was over.

Jane Lawrence, a young woman some three or four years
younger than myself, was being courted openly now by Sir
Ralph; they had eyes for no one else, and often, during those
warm siesta hours when most of the Nepalese were drowsing
under the shade of trees and tall rhododendrons, I would see
Sir Ralph, in his neat khaki shirt and pants tucked inside the

dusty leather boots, and with a net and basket and a book open in his hands, walk away with Jane by his side, a wide leghorn hat of straw on her head. There were many species of birds in these hills and along the sandy banks of the river we followed daily, with the elephants crossing and recrossing the sometimes deep treacherous water. Jane was very enthusiastic whenever Sir Ralph would point out the delicate hedge sparrow, or the rose-colored finches, and she often had her mother birdwatching too.

For the most part, I found myself alone and into my thoughts, deeply puzzled by Lindsey's involvement with Lord Gordon, and her obvious interest in Bianca's fate. On several occasions, I had overheard her voice this tragic fate to Lady Jennifer, though not in Lord Gordon's presence. She spoke as if she knew for certain that Bianca was dead.

I seldom saw Lindsey alone during those days; she did not barge into my tent as she had done that first night, yet it seemed as if she were deliberately avoiding me. Certainly, I felt she intended I was not to be much alone with Lord Gordon, for there was hardly a time when I did not see them together, except on the occasions I saw him walking and talking with the Prime Minister. Once, I saw the Rani and Guggun Singh talking with Lord Gordon and the Prime Minister. Rarely did I see the Rani during the daytime, but several times I'd glimpsed the two of them walking in the cool of the evening side by side, with their servants close in attendance and the Gurkhas always nearby.

So it was that a week later we arrived in the incredible Pokhara Valley, with spectacular range of Annapurna rising to the north, and the sharp-crested Machha Puchhare—the fishtailed mountain whose summit was split by a crevice into two curved forms which we could see clearly as we approached this magnificent scene. The morning after our arrival, the sun rose clear in the sky, and the great mountains reared their crests in the bright morning glow. It was an unforgettable sight; we could see the massive giants of the Himalayas rise, those sheer, snowy peaks of the Annapurna range shine like polished silver.

That same evening, they were aflame in the glow of the setting sun, their crests hidden behind great plumes of vermilion clouds. As soon as the tents were being pitched, I snatched Mark up and raced out to the high meadow where rape blossoms stood as a bold yellow shield beneath the great giants.

"Miss Tawny!" I glanced up as I turned my head to see Lord Gordon standing over us. I had not heard him approach, but I knew a sudden lifting in my heart.

"May I join you? I must confess that I followed you here, for I wanted to look at the baby Mark." He didn't wait for my invitation, but sat down cross-legged, and lifted Mark on his lap.

The pleasure in his expression as he looked at Mark surprised even me, for I saw a tenderness, and I had to admit that I had believed him to be callously indifferent toward his nephew during these past days.

"He looks so healthy," he commented suddenly. "A very sturdy little boy, wouldn't you say so, Miss Tawny?" I heard a trace of pride I hadn't seen before, and I smiled.

"No doubt about it, Lord Gordon," I laughed. "Mark is a perfect specimen of health. Chanda looks after him well."

"And you look after him very well indeed, too, I've noticed. I want to . . . thank you for this. It helps to know that someone like yourself has taken an interest in his well-being. I've been watching how you go off with him each morning and evening. I have wanted to join you, but there are occasions like those when I feel certain that you wanted to be on your own with him."

I felt a glow of pride wash over me, staining my cheeks, and I was grateful for the late sun's redness, for it helped to hide my feelings. Mark was laughing and kicking his fat bare feet as his uncle lifted him in the air.

"If you like, you are free to join us, Lord Gordon, anytime. I know Bianca would want you to get to know Mark. She counted on it, I believe," I said, and then I stopped, finding his eyes were searching my face.

"Thank you. I would like that, very much." His voice was

deep and I thought I saw a trace of wistful hope beneath the arrogant manner he bore at all times.

We were silent for a while, listening to the muted distant sounds of camp life, and the warblers that sang in the high still meadow.

Then I said, "I haven't given you the letters and documents which David Markus wanted me to give to you, Lord Gordon. And those which Bianca also entreated me to hand over to you. Perhaps you should have them now."

"Do you have them with you?" He had placed Mark down in the crook of his arm, a polite look of disinterest in his eyes as I nodded. "They could well be safer in your possession until we get to Kathmandu, Miss Tawny." He glanced around us in the high golden meadow even as I did, for I suddenly had the un-canny sense of being watched. I believe he must have felt that too, although he didn't voice it, and neither did I.

Inclining my head to one side, I spoke decisively. "Perhaps you ought to take a look," I insisted, and I stood up, turned my back to him, lifted my skirt and untied the strings around my waist which held the pouches in safe pockets in the lining of my petticoat, and which I wore at all times. I removed them and turned back to him.

As I sat down, I gave him the pouches and took Mark, and placed him in my lap, then said, "You must have a look. I don't want to be the only one of us responsible for all of this." I gestured to the black leather pouch which had David Markus's initials on it. Then I turned and looked out into the sunset, not speaking while he opened and read all the letters and documents which David had wanted him to have.

The sun sank slowly, leaving in its wake an illumination which touched the rape flowers and caught us up into the sud-den and special yellow world of the moment; time seemed sus-pended, breathless, like an eternity. We were quiet, and I felt his nearness with such an excruciating throb of joy and pain. If I ever knew that something was lacking in my life, I felt it more keenly in that moment with the baby close to me, and his not being mine, and the knowledge that I knew in my heart that I now loved Lord Gordon Harding and that he would never return that love for he belonged to Lindsey, and would never be free for me.

Was this then to be my punishment for having been too free with my love in my youth? Was I never to know complete happiness? I found myself hugging Mark to me, knowing that he would have my love and protection as long as he needed it.

This was dangerous, treacherous thinking, and I had to curb it; I knew I should have to turn Mark over to his uncle very soon, and supposing Bianca didn't come back? He would have Lord Gordon, and—my heart sank at this last thought—Lindsey would be the woman who would be there to influence him.

I buried my face into the baby's sweet person, all too aware that I had already become too attached to Mark, and I ached in that sadness of knowing.

"You are very sad for some reason," Lord Gordon's voice broke in on my thoughts. "And it's my guess that you are thinking of Bianca and Mark." He sighed heavily, and I turned, glad of the sudden shadow, but somehow stirred because he had seen what I could be feeling. "Don't be," he said suddenly. "Don't be sad. If . . . it is true that she may not come back, then we shall face Mark's future, and what is best for him. I must say, his father was . . . quite a man. Thank you, Tawny. For caring and for bringing to me these letters." He gestured toward the papers. "It clears everything." He stuffed them back into the pouches.

I was conscious of the fact that he'd spoken my name with something like a caress and it sent little slivers of delight through my blood, causing a strange pulsating inside me. I gave my attention to Mark, so that Lord Gordon wouldn't see how I felt, and he said:

"I will keep the letters to read over, but I do think it would be to our advantage if you used your *safe* . . . hiding place for these valuables. Just for a few days longer, until we reach Kathmandu. Do you mind very much, Tawny?"

I looked up and met his eyes; I saw a trace of amusement on

his sensuous mouth, and there was laughter in the way he was looking at me. I reddened, but I said I didn't mind, and took the pouches again.

While he took Mark, I adjusted the pouches once more to their pockets of safekeeping, and then turned again to face him. "I'm not so sure I like the idea of being responsible for these valuables, Lord Gordon. I can't think that I've seen the last of Khan Shayet, not after his having pursued me so far. He is unscrupulous, and he has murdered too many men already—"

"Please, Tawny," he broke in and I sat down facing him. "You must not be afraid of Khan Shayet, even if we haven't seen the last of him. I promise you this. You and Mark are safe with me. I have my reasons for believing that those valuables are safer with you in this caravan, and it's for only a few more days. You must trust me."

He reached out his hand and took my own, and in that one touch, I knew a new burst of joy that sounded like an explosion inside me somewhere. "You see, I just believe that things will have a way of sorting themselves out for the best. I want you to accept this too, Tawny." He kept my hand in his, and in doing so, pulled me a little closer, and our faces were very close. His lips brushed mine ever so gently so that it was like a breath, rather than a kiss.

"Gordon! Gordon?" We shot apart as Lindsey ran across the now shadowed meadow toward us. Her eyes moved over the blanket we sat on, from Gordon to myself and to the baby which he still held.

She moved over to where Gordon sat and kneeled down. "Oh, darling! What a precious charming little boy! May I hold him?" She reached for him, and my heart trembled with anxiety. But Mark began to cry, and it seemed like a shock to her. Lord Gordon stood up, holding him next to his shoulder and patting his back. He hushed immediately.

I stood up. "It's time for his feeding. Perhaps I should be getting back," I said, picking up the blanket and folding it.

"It's time we all should be back," Lord Gordon said, and I made a move to take Mark, but he said, "Allow me to carry him, won't you, Tawny? It's the least I can do for . . . Toby's son." And he winked at me full, while Lindsey came up to his side, falling into stride easily enough, as we started back.

"It seems I did arrive at a crucial time then, for him," she said, and in a most congenial manner, which rather surprised me. "It seems you have a marvelous way with babies, especially this one. His name is Mark, isn't it? He has taken to you, darling, and very much so." And I saw her smile up at Mark.

I fell in step beside Lord Gordon as we three walked across the deepening shadowed field through the rape blossoms, and back toward the bustling camp, and where the elephants were herded down by the lake to wash themselves; their bellowing screams sounded eerie in the near-twilight, and dust motes from the trail rose lightly to swirl in a soft violet cloud around the gray beasts. Smoke from the cooking fires rose too in the dusk, and away on a hill, the drums and gongs of a temple called the Buddhist faithful to prayer.

As we neared the elephants, Lord Gordon turned Mark around to face them. The baby's large blue eyes stared in delight and wonder, and Uncle looked down proudly at his nephew and chuckled. "This doesn't mean a thing to you now, Mark, but in a few years, it will." And he seemed to take pleasure himself in that thought, and my heart wrung with a new little pain for all that lay ahead.

"Oh, Gordon! You would make a splendid father. Little boys do have that natural inclination for animals, and you'd see to it that they had their share of it, I'm sure. Now, you must let me take him, while he is happy. Tawny? You don't mind so much, do you?"

I was not smiling now, but I could hardly refuse her, and I shrugged my shoulders, and Gordon gave him up rather hesitantly, I thought. Lindsey took Mark and smiled down into his laughing face.

"Cheer up, Tawny," Lord Gordon turned to me. "When we get to Kathmandu, Toby could surprise us both and be there waiting." He touched my shoulder gently with his hand, patting it reassuringly. I could feel his touch burning my skin under the faded-yellow cotton shirt; it was like a flame scorching. I met his eyes, and I thought he was amused.

I had the absurd little thought that he was laughing at Lindsey, but Lindsey turned to us both, holding Mark close to her, and she was smiling. "Oh, but that would be ever so wonderful for you, Tawny. I understand that you haven't seen him for some months—" But it was Lord Gordon who interrupted her.

"In fact, Tawny tells me that it was July. It was July, wasn't it? That he left you in Leh, Tawny?" He lifted his brows, and I marveled at the fabrication.

"Yes. Of course, it was July that he left me with Mark. These weeks . . . seem to have a way of running into months, and I lose track of time."

"Then Toby will discover for himself just how much Mark has grown, if, as you believe, Gordon, dear, he is there waiting to surprise us. How fortunate if your little sister, Lady Bianca, could be there too! Oh, Gordon! I know you are still upset over her disappearance, for that *is* what it amounts to, now, isn't it?"

Mark began to fret, and I reached over to take him, and she gave him up reluctantly, saying in his ear, to which she pressed her lips, "I believe we shall get to know each other quite well, baby Mark! Auntie Lindsey already adores you." She brushed her gown off where he'd been nestled, pleased with herself to give her attention now to the man she was planning to marry.

I could have cried. Lord Gordon looked down at Lindsey and smiled. "And Bianca could possibly show up there herself, my dear Lindsey. She has a certain streak about her that somehow always wins. If she disappeared, it was for a reason. Thank God for that." He laughed, turning away, and we began walking toward the tents.

I was uneasy; a sense of foreboding would not set my mind and heart free. It puzzled me greatly that Lord Gordon did not trust Lindsey with the truth. Especially since I knew they were planning to get married. So why? And why did he trust me? He walked between us, and Lindsey was holding onto his arm.

"I'm glad you are so optimistic, Gordon. About Lady Bianca, I mean," she said lightly. "Personally, I do think our Tawny knows more than she is revealing to us about her strange disappearance. Really, Tawny! You have been most secretive. Or have you revealed what you know already to Gordon?" She lifted her brows, amused, and it quite took my breath away that she could speak so directly, and he didn't seem upset over it at all. I had another absurd little thought that he liked this game-playing, for that is what it seemed between them.

He chuckled. "My dear Lindsey. You have a vivid imagination if you think *our* Tawny would reveal any secrets, either to you or to me. In fact, I believe you are the most secretive of the three of us, for you haven't said just why you have this morbid interest in my sister's behavior. Come now. Confess it all—"

"Lord Gordon! Oh, I say, Lord Gordon!" At the interruption, we looked up to see Sir Ralph striding toward us from another direction. He was holding a strange feathered bird in his hands, and for all the world looking abstractedly content. Jane was beside him, her face glowing with the same look.

"I say, Lord Gordon! Would you mind having a look at this species? I believe I have found a rare one, and I must have a second opinion. Do have a look."

The bird was dead, shot; it was perhaps the size of a mockingbird or a small thrush. Lord Gordon, whom I hadn't known was keen on naturalists' finds, looked it over carefully in his hands.

Sir Ralph said: "I believe it is called *Acanthoptila nepalensis*."

"Or the spiny babbler," Lord Gordon agreed. "Yes. You are right, Sir Ralph. It's my guess that you have a rare species here." And he began to examine it more closely. Jane and Lindsey crowded in to look, and I took this moment to slip away unnoticed back to my tent.

After I had given Mark his bath, a nightly ritual I'd begun to take on with great pleasure, I gave him to Chanda's care to

feed him and put him to sleep. Then I had a bath, and began
to ready for dinner. I wished desperately for a pretty, decent
gown to change into, but I had to be content with the one I
had worn every evening for the past week, and knew I should
count myself fortunate for this one.

I wanted to hold off my thoughts for a while, simply because
I did not want to destroy that tender but sweet and brief moment in the meadow. I knew that I could never allow my heart
to entertain such a presumptuous dream that he had felt what
I knew my heart had known; for him, he could be playing a
game with me, just as he was playing one with Lindsey. She
was the one he would marry; she was the one he would share
his life with, and in the end, if Bianca did not survive, it would
be Lord Gordon and Lindsey who should take Mark into their
keeping.

I was in love with Gordon Harding, and I knew it. It was a
stark and naked truth, and I put the hairbrush I was using
down beside me as I stared into that small square mirror. I
couldn't help the sigh that escaped me.

Lindsey Ash Pearson. Why did it have to be her, all over
again? I wanted to weep. Suddenly, I felt Chanda's hands on
my hair, and she began brushing it in strong strokes, and I
glanced into the mirror and saw her face behind me.

"You want I make new gown? Yes?" She smiled with a wide
clean smile, her eyes brilliant. I didn't answer her until she had
wound my hair into place and pinned on the familiar blossoms,
this time a white jasmine cluster.

Then she moved swiftly and silently across the carpeted tent
floor to her own bundle. With a swift movement, she brought
out an incredible length of silk, honey-colored white, with a
border of amber and deep brown print. It was a sari.

She brought it over to me, smiling proudly. "You have.
Keep, for you. I make"—she gestured to my own gown—"how
you like." Her earrings made small clinking sounds as she stood
back with pride.

"Chanda. How perfectly beautiful! What lovely silk!" I
touched it, feeling its smoothness between my fingers, knowing

that even the colors were rare as a jewel. "Where did you get this?"

"I . . . make friend." She smiled shyly, and I realized that I had been seeing a tall handsome Sikh, with a white turban worn over his hair and sporting an attractive black beard, lingering around the tent after the unpacking of the elephants. Of course. He was one of the elephant drivers.

She wanted me to have it, and I believed her; I knew too, that before the next day would end, her nimble fingers would have a marvelous creation made up for me.

I stood up. "Chanda. You are a kind person. Yes. I will accept this, and with thanks." I was moved deeply by her knowledge of what she'd seen in me, and that she would give her own mistress a lovely length of silk like this one. I had a vision of Lindsey's smart gowns, of Lady Jennifer's pale silks with their cream laces, and of Jane's fresh pastels of sprigged muslin which she could change into every evening. Then I recalled with a poignant longing my own choices of gowns, which I had left in my house sitting above Dal Lake in faraway Kashmir.

But this length of silk which Chanda would make for me would be special and exquisite because Chanda wanted me to have it, and because I knew myself to be in love and because I knew it would make a difference. "Yes. Thank you, Chanda," I said in a low voice, and I was aware that I had pleased her very much.

*

I was right; Chanda had the silk made up for me by the next evening, for she worked on it throughout the following day's journey, in the box atop our elephant. But it was much later than usual when we made camp, and the Rani's steward came around to inform us that no special dinner would be made this night, as it was imperative to reach Kathmandu on the following night. He warned us that we should be ready to pack and leave before dawn.

It threw the whole camp into its worst chaos; there was no organization, and the Asian voices pitched to a crescendo for what seemed like hours. It was already dark, and everyone had to shift for himself for the evening meal, around a large campfire.

Thus I was holding Mark in my lap while Chanda went to fetch her own food and Jaseen's, when Lord Gordon put his head through the door flap and said, "Is it convenient for me to come in?" He was smiling, looking rather tanned in the flare of the lantern light. My heart did a strange little turnover, for I was glad that he was here, and I had to curb my voice as I said, "Come, please do. Mark isn't asleep just yet."

He was so tall that he almost had to stoop even standing, so he sat down on a cushion across from me, and he took Mark into his arms. "I'm growing quite fond of this little fellow. Do you think he recognizes me?" He was showing his pleasure in the baby, and I had to laugh.

"Oh, I'm sure of it. The first words he will babble out will be 'Unkie Gordy' or something intelligible like so!"

"It will be cheeky of him if he does! I'll have to teach him proper English. I'll have no familiarity with the lad!" But he laughed and continued to look so very smug and pleased, chucking the baby under his fat little chin so that he laughed.

We sat there for some long minutes, taking pleasure in this beautiful child of Bianca's, and I was aware of the pleasure I had, too, in Lord Gordon's company.

"The Rani seems to be in a great hurry to reach Kathmandu," I said after a moment's silence. "Is this usual?"

He hugged Mark tightly, then settled him into the crook of his arm. "It is as usual on any caravan the Rani is on. Her impulsive moods create havoc at any given whim, as you've witnessed," he grinned darkly. Then he lowered his voice.

"There is a rumor, and I'm certain there are grounds for it, that the sudden rush to get back to the palace is because she doesn't trust the maharaja. Her spies are everywhere, as well as his are, you see. I fear we are in for something big. Last year's assassination of the Prime Minister was only the beginning. It's not hard to see which way the wind is blowing."

"What do you think might happen? Is she so powerful that

she can overrule her own husband, the hereditary Emperor of Nepal?" I frowned, recalling to mind what Lady Jennifer had already told me.

He shrugged. "It is all sliding toward a major eruption, of course. Jung Bahadur Rana is simply wooing her for a bid to take over that power she has achieved with the help of her family and the young men she collects like butterflies in a net. It all has the drama and the usual court intrigue of the old Chinese dynasties, from which she descended." He seemed careful of not saying too much, I had the impression, as he leaned back on a leather pack. But he was relaxed, and easy company to be with.

"Then it's true that the Prime Minister did have the Emperor's Minister assassinated, or rather, through the Rani's plot to gain control?" I asked.

He nodded. "We naturally believe it at the residency. It's all a political move, of course. The British are in on it." He didn't even sound apologetic for our government's intervention.

"So your guess is that Nepal is rushing toward a new regime, backed by the British, and quite like the way Ladakh was overthrown," I said with quiet speculation.

He smiled with a trace of bitternesss on his lips. "Hopefully without so much bloodshed, or without the overwhelming greed of one general. Jung Bahadur Rana could bring much to this country's welfare. It is almost a sure thing that the old regime of the family of the present maharaja is coming to a close."

We both reflected on this for a small time; I found it rather sad, knowing an era was coming to a final ending, even though the era had been one of corruption and greed, as this one was notorious for being.

"There is so much about you that I'd like to know," he said softly, "like now. You are the most incredible woman I've ever met. Gavin told me something about you, but I could not have imagined you like this." His eyes were suddenly all over my face, warm and reading me. The shaft of light so yellow from the lantern fell across his face, and he was close to me. The baby had fallen asleep in the crook of his arm, and although he hadn't moved, the space between us seemed intimate.

If this very nearness aroused such a tumult of desire within me each time I was close to him, I knew this was a mistake, because I knew that Lindsey was in the picture. My heart was beating so fast that I felt giddy, in spite of that fact.

Yet no matter how I tried, I could not pry my eyes from his; they were devouring me as if he were seeing me for the first time. He did not touch me as he had yesterday in that high meadow among the rape blossoms. But this was more than a touch; it said everything and did everything I wanted to know and feel.

We heard the gentle coughs outside the tent, and the moment was gone. Chanda came in softly, after speaking to Jaseen, and Lord Gordon glanced smilingly at her. She understood, and took Mark and placed him down on the pallet where she slept with him. Lord Gordon stood up then and turned to me as I, too, stood up.

"It will be an early start, and the day will be very long tomorrow. But when we do reach the capital, I will take you to the residency. I will leave you now. Try to get as much sleep as you can. Good night, Tawny."

And he was gone, out into the night.

Lying restlessly on my pallet that night, I tried to banish the memory of that moment when everything had become clear and answered. I thought what a fool I was. Within my heart I had faced up to the truth that I loved him; for Toby I had felt gratitude, peace and even companionship—a safe place for a once scorched heart to be.

But now, I knew I was going forward into something that would inevitably only make it far worse when the day of reckoning came. There was Lindsey—hadn't she been there in that long-ago time? Every instinct of survival told me that I ought to bow out before I was caught in that web all lovers found themselves enmeshed in, and every fiber of my being rebelled to fight for what could be mine. They were not yet married, and I rolled that over in mind. I was no mere nineteen-year-old love-sick girl now for Lindsey to use and frighten. Perhaps now Lindsey and I were on a common battleground. But that was treacherous ground; the bitter gall rose up in my mouth as I remembered just how Lindsey always got what she wanted, and I knew she wanted Gordon Harding.

And once she learned that Mark was Bianca's child, what would she do? My concern for Mark's well-being was most important. This was reality, not my foolish dreams. I pulled myself together and found comfort that Lindsey did not even suspect that Mark was not my own son. There was time enough to cross that bridge, and so I went to sleep after tossing and turning through the hours before dawn.

10

It was midafternoon when our caravan entered through the Chandragiri Pass, and to the east, Kathmandu lay out before us, a perfected Shangri-La, with its sacred rivers winding through the heart, shining blue ribbons in the mellow hazy sunlight. To the left, the great Buddhist shrine of Swayambhu Nath rose high on a hill, its sacred chaitya a gilded parasol glittering in the sun, and beneath it, a pair of eyes on each of its four walls to signify the all-seeing power of the godhead. It sheltered the world's largest gold image of Buddha, some two thousand years old.

To me, Kathmandu was the very essence of an Oriental Shangri-La, mystic and forbidden to the outside world. Visitors had to be invited to enter into this kingdom, and with a strange feeling of awe, I knew I was one of the fortunate outsiders, and I had no little thrill of anticipation.

Our caravan was a most splendid spectacle reserved for only royalty as we made our way into this lovely old city of temples and pagodas, quite unlike anything I'd yet experienced. They were designed by Newar, who had built the famous White Pagoda in faraway Peiping, Lady Jennifer informed me.

The Queen demanded pomp and ceremony, and all of her train was decked out in glittering array like that of a medieval court, with the fanfare of trumpets and hide drums going before us, scattering the great swarm of people. Those who came down from the hills with their great burdens on their backs, and the long file of coolies, who carried everything in and out of Nepal, ran along either side of the caravan of elephants.

The streets were broad leading down into Durbar Square,

THE JADE PAGODA   147

where the palace was located, and from my perch in the box atop the great gray beast, I caught glimpses of the narrow, tortuous back streets, which were a fascinating jumble of old houses with elegantly carved figures on their wooden posts and window sills. There were tiny shops beneath the two- and three-story houses, where the shopkeepers sat in beautifully kept wooden stalls, on small carpets, weighing and measuring their grains and spices, selling vegetables, fruits, milk, cheese, chickens and eggs, as well as firewood and bright-colored cloth. There were chang stalls too, where one could have that hot tea the Nepali loved so well, on those back streets and where throngs of people this late afternoon had come to stare in amazement at the elephants entering through the gates to the palace courtyard.

I had time to glance around in that huge courtyard before the utter chaos of unpacking began; it was paved in brick, and I saw that if these elephants could all lumber inside it, then it must be massive, and it was. Directly through the most beautifully carved wooden gates was the entrance to the palace itself, with the huge dragons guarding either side. The palace, white and glittering in the colorful glowing light of the westerly sun, was massive, and unlike the ancient castles and fortresses I'd known in Kashmir and Hunza.

This was indeed fashioned on the scale of the Chinese style, and I found I liked it. The elephants were lined up before the massive gates, and in turn, sank down on their knees for the disembarking amid the shouting and confusion of the drivers, the servants and the porters.

It was about an hour later that I found myself with Mark in my arms, riding in a rickshaw with Chanda beside me, following the other members of our small English party, leaving the palace, and headed toward the British residency. The purple of the early evening had set in, and racing along between the high rosy brick walls of the narrow streets the coolies ran through, I had glimpses of the flaming passion trees, of lush banana fronds and beautiful old houses set in well-kept gardens, like small palaces beyond locked gates.

At last we reached the compound, which was not far from the Durbar Square; indeed, it was adjacent to one of those incredible temples, around which was a constant beehive of a marketplace, in which life and death was side by side.

Once inside the compound, however, it was like arriving in a different world—a paradise of flowers, fountains and quiet air of the English. I was amazed as the rickshaw boy ran up the curving drive and halted in front of a long two-story white house with a red tiled roof. Beyond in the grounds, I caught glimpses of small bungalows, and I guessed that the British citizens who served out here would most likely be keen on our arrival.

But even as we tumbled out of our rickshaws, bag and baggage littering the wide front verandah, only the Nepali porters came out to attend us. Immediately, however, Lady Jennifer was swept off to her private quarters with her daughter, giving hurried invitations at a later hour for cool drinks in her parlor, and Lindsey too, disappeared quickly, somehow aloof. I saw Sir Ralph take his hurried leave and two coolies following him with the rickshaw, taking all of his gear, retreating to the grounds somewhere.

I was left with Lord Gordon, and he gave explicit instructions to the porters to take our baggage to his quarters. "I think it best if you lodge with me, Tawny. For the time being. Never mind the rushed decision. God alone knows what has taken place since I left here three months ago! Come along. There's plenty of room."

We went through a wide doorway into a cool hall that divided the wings of this rather large house, and we went through this hall to the back, which opened onto a gallery overlooking a lovely garden court, around which the three other wings of the house were built.

Lord Gordon's quarters were on the lower floor, a very large suite of rooms that were spacious and as cool as that garden itself was, with wide windows covered with netting of deep green as a protection against the insects. There was a large lounge, with chintz-covered sofas and chairs, and deep Persian carpets over the wide floors made it quiet and comfortable and more like an English house than I could have imagined.

I glanced around the room, suddenly enjoying the luxurious sight before me, yet all I wanted to do was to sink into a bath of warm scented water and relax!

Lord Gordon had seen the expression on my face and he smiled. "I know you must be as weary of travel as I am, Tawny. So without further fuss, I'll take you to your rooms—you may have the one with the small dressing room, and the bath." He laughed.

I followed him down a corridor, and into the rooms. "One of the maids will be along to do for you. Jaseen can act as your houseboy, so as not to refute my houseboy's status," he smiled. "There are beds in the servants' quarters for him. Chanda can remain with you, naturally."

"This is more than I expected," I said in a low voice. "It's all so incredibly English." I had to laugh, glancing around the large bedroom.

"Yes. The British invariably will have their piece of England wherever they lodge! I trust you will be comfortable here."

"Oh, I shall, of course." I laughed again rather weakly, recalling the inconvenience I'd had for the past year! I turned to face him. He seemed hesitant to leave me.

"Make use of the hot water, and then, later we shall go join Sir Henry and Lady Jennifer for those drinks. Tomorrow, we shall have another command performance duty at the Palace. Don't forget it. Meanwhile, I must go look into the office. Perhaps there will be some word or message waiting for us."

"I hope so. And, thank you . . . for this," I said softly, gesturing to the room with one hand.

"Don't mention it. When you're ready, just come into the lounge. I have a study, too, if you should need to write letters. It's to the far side, adjacent to my bedroom. Please feel free to make this your home."

His thoughtfulness overwhelmed me, and the warmth in his dark smoke-gray eyes was like a soft caress on my face. I wanted to weep and to laugh and to sing all at once, so I hid my face into Mark's curls. "Thank you. You are . . . generous." I could barely get the words out, and I knew I didn't want him to leave either. But the porters brought in my bags, and servants began carrying in great copper pails of steaming water.

So it was just as well that he went to the door and smiled back at me, then left.

*

It some two hours later that I—shampooed, scrubbed, scented and relaxed as I'd not been for weeks—months even— sat before the wide screened window, buffing my broken nails, feeling elegant in the new silk gown Chanda had created for me. I was waiting for Lord Gordon to put in an appearance.

Mark had been given a bath and fed, and was sleeping in the small dressing room where Chanda would stay also, and I had come into the lounge, hoping that I should find my host waiting for me. But he had not returned from his office, the house-boy informed me. Even he went out, and I found a comfort-able place beside the window.

I had hardly given thought to my brother, Gavin, for some time, and suddenly a great longing to see him overwhelmed me; a rush of tears came to my eyes, and I brushed them aside, willing myself not to cry now to redden my eyes. How brief had been that moment that we'd both been caught up in the drama of the rescue in Khan Shayet's camp that night! It was more like an unreality—some nightmare I might have gone through. But to have seen him for that moment, and to know he was alive, had been a joy I'd been unprepared for.

David Markus had told me, only hours before I'd seen Gavin, that my brother was not dead, and all that happened in the wake of that telling had been foresight on his part. How strange it was to remember, and to know he had sacrificed all! A deep sigh escaped me, for I thought of Toby and even with that thought, I wondered what might have been had things turned out differently that blizzardly night! I bit my underlip now, thinking that I could never have loved Toby as I knew my heart was already lost to Gordon Harding!

Would I ever see my brother or Toby again? Something Gordon had said two nights ago gave me reason to think he knew more on the whole affair than what I was led to believe he did; certainly, I knew nothing more than what had taken place that late-October night crossing the Karakoram Mountains.

A sudden shiver of apprehension brought goose pimples to my skin when I recalled what Gordon had said of Khan Shayet; he felt as I'd felt, that I hadn't seen the last of this big Kirghiz. Even now, I wore those valuables beneath this silk gown, in between the petticoats and tucked inside two side pockets, for safekeeping.

And then I had to laugh at my fears; what could Khan Shayet do now? I was secure with Mark, safe in his uncle's rooms, within the British compound, and Gurkha soldiers guarding the gates.

A vision of Bianca's face came to me; and I knew a grief that would take me a long time to get over as I remembered her all through those weeks and months in Nazar Shah's little home. Oh, that there would be word of her safety! I longed to know, and I stood up suddenly, and turned back to the room.

I was not prepared to see Lindsey standing there. I had to blink twice; I had not heard her enter; indeed, I had heard no sound at all. It caused me to tremble almost violently in that split second when our eyes met across the deep shadowy twilight of the room.

Never had I seen her look so attractive as she did now; the blue silk gown she wore had a gossamer sheen about it, and the way it folded across her high full breasts gave her a seductress look. Even her fine white skin had a luminous glow, and her hair was as glossy as sealskin.

"You startled me, Lindsey! I had no idea—" I stopped, for I did not want her to see just how unnerving her presence had made me.

"Of course you didn't even suppose I'd find my way into Gordon's private rooms, Tawny dear! You seem to take no notice of anyone but yourself in these matters." She laughed huskily, so sure of herself that it brought a sharp pain to my throat.

"I don't know what you can be thinking of—" Again, she stopped me with a small gesture of her hand and then walked across the room to where I almost stood rooted, my cheeks blazing.

"You know all right, Tawny. You know very well, yet you pretend with your so-called innocent mind that Gordon is available for only you! Well, you have a lot to learn. He is not free for you to . . . throw yourself at, as you did my husband in the past! You are a little doxy, but this time you will have no chance to get as far as you did with Neil."

She did not raise her voice; every nerve of her was in control, even the smile was genuine; yet everything she was throwing at me seemed like an echo, and I ached to throw back my anger into that smooth face. But I said nothing, meeting her eyes with as much calmness as I could will.

This silence of mine seemed to agitate her; her eyes left my face for a second and then she said, "I've been in to see Mark. He is sleeping beautifully. I am here because Gordon asked me to come over. He is . . . in my rooms, you see." She moved the tip of her tongue over her lips lightly, a secretive assured manner in her every movement.

I could have died then; of course. He had gained my trust, yet he had not spoken his heart; it had been only one-sided. He was in love with this woman, not me! But he had asked me to trust him. He had given me rooms in his quarters, but he had gone to . . . Lindsey!

I heard myself saying, "You have no right whatsoever to come in and look at Mark. What concern is he of yours, pray tell?" I matched her poise, calm and defiant.

"Don't I?" She lifted her eyebrows and inclined her head sidewise, that secretive smile almost dazzling. "That is what I came over for, you see, to look in on Mark. Gordon asked me to. You see, Tawny. I know the truth now. You couldn't hide it from me forever. You told a lie about Mark being yours, but I know he is not your child. He is Bianca's son, and you have no rights to him."

"I have every right. What is so amazing is that you think you can come in like this and speak like this to me." I was angry, and I moved across the room, hurrying away from her, for the sight of this woman was insidious to me. But I almost ran to the room where I'd left Mark sleeping. She came after me.

She laughed lightly, seeing my great agonizing fear for him. He was sleeping peacefully, and Chanda was nowhere in sight.

"You can be sure of one thing. Mark is not yours, not now, not ever. His mother is dead, and Gordon and I shall raise Mark as our own. Oh, Gordon knows now, about you. He was too upset to come back here, so he asked me to look in on Mark, and to tell you in so many words that you should not put in an appearance at Sir Henry's sherry party. I believe he wants not to see you, and be reminded of his own . . . folly in trusting your character."

It was wickedly said; for the second time in my life I felt I could murder, and it was directed at this one woman!

"Get out!" I said, steeling every nerve within me to keep from striking her or raising my voice. "Get out of my sight." My eyes locked with hers, deadly defiant.

She hesitated; she seemed poised and on the brink to say something more, but suddenly, she shrugged her shoulders, and moved with grace out into the corridor and walked into the lounge. I gave one more look at the sleeping baby before I went out and closed the door. Lindsey was still in the lounge when I walked in.

"I will go now. But just so that you know this, Tawny Butler, I will say it now. Gordon and I are to be married within a few days, and Mark will remain with us, with me, and I intend to raise him as I would my own son. Don't you forget it."

I turned my back on her and went to stand by the window, looking out at nothing. She laughed, a sort of bubbling kind of laugh, and I heard the door open and close behind her.

Only then did I begin to tremble with my anger. My first

thought was for the safety of Mark. I wanted to take him away, out of the reach of this woman who I knew was my personal enemy. But where could I run to now? I had faced the certain hazards of death at the hands of Khan Shayet to bring Mark to this safe place in his uncle's care and protection. I had believed Lord Gordon, trusted him and his responsibility for Bianca's son.

I found myself pacing the floor, restless, sick with fear and hatred for what Lindsey had created. It was Lindsey who had done this thing, I thought suddenly. It was she who had deliberately come in here, perhaps to—to *goad* me into a reaction that would place Mark's life in jeopardy!

With that thought, I stopped pacing. Of course. She had wanted me to take Mark and thus give reasons for my kidnapping him! It was just like her to be so diabolically clever.

I had to give Lindsey credit for one thing: She knew Mark was not my own son, that he was Bianca's. Lord Gordon must have confided in her. Well, I thought, indignantly, I had done my duty for Mark. I had brought him to his uncle, and my duty was finished, here and now. I made up my mind I would go to Lord Gordon, face that anger he apparently was directing at me, and I should tell him that I was no longer responsible for his nephew. Then he could do whatever he liked.

The door opened before I could reach it, and Lord Gordon stood there. It was such a shock that for one split second I could find no words. He had changed from the khaki bush clothes to a most dignified suit of stiff white linen, the shirt beneath the jacket a cool pearl gray. His beard was trimmed, and his ruddy hair glistened from the obvious bath he'd had. Oh, yes, I thought with a bitter contemptuousness, he had made himself more at home in Lindsey's presence, and I detested him as I knew I did her.

He looked at me with a secretive smile, and moved across the room to look closely at me. "If I didn't know better, Tawny"— his voice was low, somehow guarded—"I'd say you are a very distressed young woman, but a very beautiful one. What has happened? Is Mark—" He stopped, glancing quickly toward the bedroom.

"He is sleeping peacefully," I said, a strange ache in my throat. "I'm waiting for Chanda, but I would like to talk with you, Lord Gordon." I tried to keep my voice impersonal, distant.

"Of course. I too want a talk with you. I'm sorry I took so long. I had Pemba bring over my clothes and I had a good wash in my office. I felt that I had all of Asia in my hair and clothes! Come. Let's make ourselves comfortable."

This caught me by surprise. "I am sorry that I chased you out of your quarters . . ." I bit my underlip, disquieted more than ever.

"My dear Tawny. You did not chase me out. It was just more convenient to have my hot water brought there. Sir Henry was not yet available, and tonight, I shall see him. I am ready now, presentable enough, I hope, to take a most beautifully gowned young woman to dine with me at the senior resident's supper party." We had stood facing each other, and now, he gestured for me to sit down in the comfortable armchair. Then he took the deep chair across from me. "You are a most enchanting creature in that lovely gown, Tawny."

This most delightful compliment took me unawares. Hadn't he sent Lindsey over to me to say I was not to put in an appearance at Sir Henry's party? I hardly knew where to begin. Yet I knew I could not be subjected to such torment as I would be suffering if I stayed here and watched the man I loved marry a woman like Lindsey Pearson! I wanted to be firm, distant, but instead I thanked him.

"The gown was of Chanda's making and her gift to me," I said, so pleased that he had taken notice. "I must admit, I have very few suitable clothes for this climate. It was generous on her part to have somehow bargained for it on the caravan, don't you think so?"

The pleasure was immediately in his expression. "I'd say it was most loyal of Chanda. She is a valuable asset to us—to you and Mark, and to me. Now. What did you have in mind to talk with me?" He sat back, comfortable, looking more relaxed and so handsome that my heart began to hammer madly inside me.

My voice, when I spoke, was tight and unlike my own. "Lord Gordon. I made a promise to your sister and to her husband that I should do what I could do in bringing their son to you. I tried hard to bring Bianca to you, but the circumstances, which you know by now, were out of my control. But I have done my duty, and I feel that I should now be relieved of . . . all obligations. I believe it is time now that I should make other arrangements, and then I should like to return to Kashmir as quickly as possible, before the snows come."

He seemed genuinely stunned. "Tawny. I—I believed you were concerned for Mark's welfare?"

"I am. Oh, but I am! I have brought him here to your keeping, and since you will be marrying very soon, I think that Mark will have all the security which I could not continue to give him." My face was hot, my hands cold.

He was silent, and the shadows gathered in the quiet room, but neither of us thought of lighting the lamp.

He stared at me, his eyes burning like coals over my face. "I see. I had no idea you felt so strongly. I beg you, my dear Tawny, to bear with me for just a while longer, until I can settle everything. Mark needs both of us right now. Can you not see your way to remain with us for an indefinite period?" He was not laughing at me, but spoke so seriously that it wrung my heart.

I shook my head. I was near to tears, for when he talked like this, I became gullible. "Lindsey would resent my being here, as well as you should know."

He frowned. His eyebrows went up. "Lindsey? Whatever has she to do with all of this?"

Of course I felt like a fool, but a surprised one. "She knows about Mark, but then, I suppose she was entitled to know—"

"Entitled? But however did she know? How could she know about Mark?"

"Why, you told her, didn't you? After all, she will be your

wife in a few days—" I stopped, for never had I seen such a black angry look.

He jumped up. "Did she tell you this? When?"

I hadn't meant to bring her name into all this; I had meant to be calm and hard, coldly asking to be relieved of a duty I had completed above and beyond the call, somehow reminding myself vaguely of those words on a printed sheet of paper in that letter he himself had written to me.

But he grabbed my hands and pulled me to my feet, facing him.

"When? When did she tell you this?"

"She came . . . here, not more than—" I stopped, for his eyes bored into my own, and his fingers gripped my shoulders, but I hardly felt them.

"Damn Lindsey! Do you think I care a rush for her?"

"You are engaged to her—"

"Not that I know of. But, how did she learn of Mark's parents?"

"Did you not tell her?"

"I did not. God in heaven! She was the last person I wanted to know about Mark!"

"I don't understand. She has implied all along that you and she—" He stopped me with his fingers touching my lips gently.

"To hell with Lindsey and what she has implied! It's you I care about, my dearest Tawny! And we'll get this settled right now." What I read in his eyes that moment, nothing else in the whole world mattered. He was not in love with Lindsey, nor was he going to marry her!

His arms went around me suddenly, and his mouth came down on mine. It was sweet to respond to him with an abandon that matched his own, but only for an instant. I did not want to be swept off my feet for a second time; it was a lesson I had had to pay for and dearly so. I had suffered painfully with Neil. I did not intend to go through it all again.

I tried to move out of his arms, but he would not let me go.

"Tawny, Tawny. Do you know what you do to me? I fell

madly in love with you when I saw you on that first day! My God! I never dreamed that I could love a woman as I know I love you." He held me back from him, looking down into me, and I was so overcome by joy and surprise that I could not speak.

"You are beautiful, now, tonight. But never more beautiful than I saw you in that morning light for the first time, with your unbound hair the color of wild honey, and your eyes a strange shade darker! A woman proud and free, and I knew something happened to my heart then. I love you, Tawny."

No words had ever meant so much to me. It was madness, but it was sweet to listen to him. His mouth came down on mine again, and I was lost in this new and dreadfully wild sweetness that made my whole body tremble.

I stepped back in his arms. "What of . . . Lindsey?" I wanted to know.

"And what about Lindsey? Who is she?" He was smiling down at me.

"You and she—"

"She means absolutely nothing to me."

"Then you are not promised to her?" I had to say it, for I simply had to know.

He shook his head. "Whatever was between us is over now, long since. Oh, yes, I know she had fanciful notions that we should be properly married, but that was totally on her part, her idea and never mine."

"She was your mistress."

"For a brief period. I was attracted to her when she first came out to Nepal, mainly because she was an Englishwoman and made herself available. She had taken a keen interest in Bianca's welfare too, and she was the one who prompted me to engage a companion for my wayward sister." His eyes were suddenly full of laughter.

"She gave you a splendid recommendation for my competent character," I said.

"She said she knew you in the past, that you would be perfect for the post. But I already knew of your character, from your brother. And, I knew your father, Sir William, enough so that he spoke of you."

"Our families are known enemies. The Butlers of Butlers Reach in Cornwall, and the Hardings of Devon, just across the border. Did he not speak of the outstanding feud existing between us?"

"Does it exist at all, except on some pages of carefully written manuscripts and in the servants' minds, who tend never to forget feuds to their dying day?" He laughed. "Your father was too wise and too gentle for that, and I don't remember anything particular that I would call you or Gavin out to account for. Oh, my darling Tawny! I do love you. Please never believe that there was anything like this between Lindsey Pearson and myself!"

"You did not go to her this evening?"

"Certainly not. I haven't seen her since we arrived. But, damn Lindsey! What I want to know is this. Do you love me, Tawny Butler, enough to marry me? Can I dare hope that you would love me?"

He was serious, unsmiling, but wickedly handsome and I was suddenly delirious with happiness bursting like tiny explosions in my heart.

"Is this true?" I whispered. "Can this be true? I do love you, Gordon. And I love you enough to be your wife."

He took my face, cupped it in his hands and kissed my lips ever so softly. "Then you have made me the luckiest and the happiest man in all this kingdom, Tawny. I have many harsh ways, as you will learn. My faults are not few. But I can promise you that, from this second on into time eternal, my heart is yours. Whatever has been before is over and finished. Will you believe this, and trust me?"

I felt as though I were dreaming, and I didn't want to awaken ever and find that it was only a dream. Does one ever want to leave such joy and bliss to face a reality that could only be dull, after such a promise of true love?

"More than life itself," I cried softly, knowing my eyes were moist with joy. "I too, have many . . . faults," I confessed in a hushed voice.

"Not many that we can't overcome together," he said, drawing me close to his chest, my head nestled there while he kissed my hair. "We shall discover everything together—a lovely voyage of discovery of each other. It will be a new beginning for both of us. Whatever faults or perfections which made our characters up until this hour, helped mold us for each other from this second onward. We shall be happy. Let us both count our blessings that we are ready for each other."

No one had ever spoken such beauty and truth as this to me before. When he kissed me then, there was comfort and reassurance which I had not been prepared for. I gave myself up to the bliss of his arms and his kisses.

"I want to announce our plans tonight, my darling Tawny! I am a man of action, and I do not propose to put off the most important thing in my life. I fear you will learn that I am a most impatient man at times." He was smiling indulgently at me. "Have you any objection to a very rushed wedding?"

"None whatsoever," I said lightly, ecstatically. "But you may forget that I am a *married woman* already, of your own making! How will the Lady Jennifer and Miss Jane, not to mention others, react to this sudden and fearfully improper announcement?" I laughed. "And I even have a baby son. And where is my dear Tobias Roberts, the missing husband?" I teased, but there was a touch of anxiety reflected in my voice, and he noticed it.

A deep chuckle escaped his throat. "I can promise you, I did not forget this situation. I have already underscored the usefulness of your married state to perfection. As far as Lady Jennifer is concerned, she is well known for her own modes of coping with any surprise situation! Do you care so very much, my dearest Tawny, about shedding the guise of being Mrs. Tobias Roberts on such short notice?" His eyes seemed to be all over my face, and I tingled with anticipation as his hands moved over my arms, warm, caressing.

I shook my head. "None whatsoever, since I haven't known

the complete bliss of that union. I can very well shed the guise easily enough. I do admit that I am very attached to Mark, and when the time comes for me to part with him, I shall know a certain heart-wrenching pain, I'm sure. But, I would gladly give him to his own mother. I do pray always that she is safe and well, and will come for her beautiful little son."

"Then that makes two of us in perfect agreement, my love. Oh, but now. Now, we must hurry on over to the bungalow. They will be wondering what has happened to us."

We left shortly, leaving Chanda in care of Mark, and Pemba and Jaseen looking after things. I am sure that none of us had even a shred of premonition of what this night was to bring.

11

It was a lovely evening when we stepped out into the exotic garden of the compound. The pagoda-like temple adjacent to the grounds was lighted with lanterns that gave off a luminous glow in the soft night. The sky was a deep pale blue with the smell of wood smoke and incense burning in the air. Muted sounds of the inevitable hide drums reached us, not loud or demanding, but serving as a background to this incredible land ruled by maharajas of ancient Chinese and Tibetan origins. We walked slowly, aware of each other and the magical mystery and wonder of our love discovered by us.

Stars were already jewel-bright in the deeper depth of the nocturnal blue, lighting our path across the garden toward the large comfortable bungalow of the resident, which was now silhouetted like a smudge of black ink, and from which soft lighted lamps glowed warmly.

As we passed a heavily scented rose enclosure, Gordon stopped and plucked a sweet-smelling yellow blossom, and gave it to me. "A rose of promise to you, my darling," he said softly kissing my cheek. It was like a signature of our declared love. The petals had not yet fully opened, and it was wet with dew folded inside the sweet perfumed heart.

I moved in a haze of happiness; beyond that haze, I knew there could be a rude reality. But here was my love beside me, looking down at me, and he took me into his arms and it seemed to be the most natural thing in the world for his mouth to find mine.

He lifted my face with both his hands, and his lips wandered lightly over my hair and my eyes and came back to my mouth, this time with such sudden and fierce strength that it made me tremble. The last shred of memory of that old past with Neil was chased away by that kiss of promise. This was something enduring, lasting until the end of time itself.

So this is love, I thought. That emotion of the heart that lifts one beyond the heights of human experience! I loved, and I was miraculously loved and by this man. I was prepared to risk everything for love such as this.

"We shall be so happy, my darling," he whispered. "Happier than either of us could ever have dreamed. It's my promise to you, and it begins right now." And I believed him.

We turned and walked hand in hand up the steps onto the wide verandah of the bungalow, which was rather large and spacious-looking, even in the night. Two very straight-looking Gurkha soldiers stood nearby, with rifles in scabbards on their backs. They nodded to Gordon, recognizing him, and we came to the wide screened doors, which was opened for us by a very correct Nepalese butler.

We entered the spacious hall, which divided the house into two wings; through the opened doors to the left was the lilting sound of someone playing the piano, and laughter floated out. From the closed double doors to the right, a man came out.

"Oh, there you are, Gordon!" he said hurrying over to us. "I was beginning to wonder what happened to keep you. But now I can see, and clearly, by Jove!"

"Sir Henry. My apologies for being late. I do want you to meet Gavin's sister, Miss Tawny Butler." Gordon spoke with pride, and it made me quite heady with the wonder and joy of it all.

"Well. This is indeed an occasion—by gad, if it's not!" His mild blue eyes widened behind his small square spectacles: a very distinguished gentleman, I thought, mentally putting him beside his wife Lady Jennifer. "Miss Butler. I am indeed honored to meet you. What we have heard of you and your illustrious brother is enough to make anyone stand up and take notice!" He took my hand in his, welcoming me warmly.

"Sir Henry," I said politely, not quite believing all I was hearing. I was not prepared for his honors.

"Sir Henry," Gordon said seriously. "Miss Tawny has just promised to become my wife, and has indeed made me the most fortunate happy man I know. You are the first to know, and I do not intend to keep it a secret or wait for more than three days before we take our vows." He smiled down at me, and I melted in that sweet heady warmth.

Feigning great surprise, Sir Henry beamed. "No! But, by gad, this is splendid, my dear fellow! Congratulations!" He shook Gordon's hand, and then kissed both my cheeks, and then my mouth hardily. "We shall have to do something about that in a very short time. But first. You both must hurry with me to my study. Before anyone else sees you. Come along. If my wife spies you, I'll never get this chance again."

He turned to the butler. "Nadar. Bring a bottle of that champagne and glasses to my study. And mind you, don't let Lady Jennifer catch you!"

The young man smiled knowingly. "Yes, sir. I know. I will do what I can." And Sir Henry laughed, placing the long thin cigar back in his mouth as we went with him toward the back of the house somewhere.

He opened the door and I entered first. There were three people inside, and I know I simply stared in utter amazed confusion. Bianca, Toby and Gavin turned to face us, and in another second, all wild emotions of the heart tore loose, and never had such a reunion been so dramatic as this!

There were tears, laughter and amazed questions to be answered; Gordon, I finally learned, had known that they were safe, but he hadn't seen them until now. This was to be his gift to me, as well as himself, and I could hardly believe it.

Bianca and Gordon met as she ran into his arms, and I was caught up by Gavin. Toby, dear loyal Toby! "How? Where? When?" I cried out, speechless except for my joy. Everyone was talking at once, and no sense could be made until Sir Henry brought order together by mixing drinks and handing them around and proposed toasts to this most incredible moment.

It was all too fantastic as their story folded out piecemeal during the next hour, which took some doing, as Sir Henry tried to keep at bay the demands of his perplexed wife, who wondered why we could not all go in to the dinner with the other guests she was having to entertain, and tell our stories there.

No one paid any attention to her demands, it seemed, and so we learned a sort of lopsided version of what actually did happen. Bianca and I fell into each other's arms and we both wept while I told her about Mark and Chanda and Jaseen and of our flight from Khan Shayet in time to meet Gordon in western Nepal.

Bianca laughed and began piecing her thread of the story. Gavin had suddenly swooped down from nowhere in the later part of May, and taken her with him to join Toby somewhere along the old China silk route in Outer Mongolia; they then made straight for Kathmandu down through Lhasa, Tibet. They had just arrived not two hours back.

It was only then that I realized that they all three were still in their travel-stained clothes, Bianca dressed in a most peculiar Tibetan skirt and jacket, with laced soft leather boots on her small feet. She looked as regal and as proud as any one of those Tibetan princesses she had been among.

Gavin said, "We were caught in one of those earth-shaking avalanches that night when we'd left the Kirghiz camp." He told us of the remarkable escape. "And if Toby had not turned back during that blinding snowstorm, I feel sure that the Hunzukut men with me would have perished, as I would have too. But the avalanche saved us from the hands of Khan Shayet that winter. We had to hole up for the greater part of the winter, and the Hunzukut men kept us alive by using many ingenious tricks. When the thaws came at last, we made for China. Toby stayed with our caravan while I went back to search out Bianca and Tawny."

Bianca laughed, and I was aware of how beautiful her laugh was. "Gavin found me ready to set out from Nazar Shah's farm, because I was so forlorn and unhappy in not hearing

from the Mir that you'd got through safely. In fact, we both
learned from the Mir that Khan Shayet had struck out toward
Leh in pursuit of a white woman! It was a fearful time. But
Gavin asked me to marry him, and the Mir blessed our marriage before we set out to join Toby. We are so happy, Tawny
dear. I hope you like the idea of my being your sister."

Nothing could have been more joyous; I fell into Gavin's
arms, excited and crying too, and Gordon was swept up with
this news as I was, while Sir Henry kept passing around our
refilled glasses.

And then Gordon made our announcement to them.
"Tawny!" Bianca cried. "You and Gordy? Oh, how marvelous.
Simply marvelous! Oh, Gordy! I am so happy for you. Tawny is
the most wonderful woman in the whole world, and I know she
will make you happy."

It couldn't have pleased me more, but Gordon said, "I know
she will make me happy, you little minx. But I can only hope I
will make her just as happy. I consider myself a very fortunate
man."

"And with this I certainly agree, Gordon," Toby said quietly,
and I turned to look at this man I might have married had fate
not intervened. And of this I was certain: Toby. Reliable,
steady Toby. I loved him in a strange but tender way, not with
the heady sweetness of my love for Gordon. He had turned
back because of fate, and had brought my brother out of certain death. And in so doing, he had opened the doors for me to
run into Gordon's love.

*

When we went in to dinner, Gavin and Bianca and Toby
declined going in, for they wanted to take advantage of hot
baths and sleep.

I don't remember much of the evening, for it whirled around
me like a myriad of color and laughter and happiness in one
great explosion. There was music and delicious food, people everywhere, wishing Gordon and me much happiness, and toasts
were drunk again and again. It was heady and sweet, and if the

champagne went to my head, who could blame me? With Gordon at my side, his hand warm on my waist, or on my elbow, or just touching my hand, I stood on that brink of discovery with him, loving every second of it. I could not break the spell that came over me each time my eyes wandered to his face and found his eyes feeding on me.

I was hardly aware of time passing; the dinner was magnificent, and there seemed to be many people, and I had no remembrance of thinking one thought of Lindsey or why she had not put in an appearance. It seemed natural enough to just not think about her.

After the dinner, Gordon and I had our first waltz together, and I felt as if I were floating in a dreamy delight as he swung me off onto the floor while the guests watched us dance the first few measures. I could feel his hand burning through the silk of my gown, his face dark and close to mine. I was deliciously giddy, and not just from the wine and champagne.

"Happy, my darling?" he said down at me. "You look ravishing. No wonder Toby was looking at you with his heart in his eyes. He loves you, you know. I saw it. Are you sure that you've chosen the right man?" There was a strange huskiness in his voice, and my heart nearly stopped beating.

"It might have been Toby, but for . . . fate. Yes. But, there are no doubts in my mind or heart about my choice. You gave me no choice, you see." I smiled.

"And I need not fear . . . losing you to him?"

"Never. You will never need fear anyone," I told him.

"Oh, my darling!" His hand tightened on my waist. "I can see that you are so good for me. I couldn't bear it if your heart were fixed on someone else. And that reminds me. I am very pleased that your brother is now my brother-in-law. At last I can feel free to say that Bianca has a husband who will answer to her peculiar needs. Let us be thankful for this."

"Yes. Oh, yes. We have so much to be thankful for," I said with a little catch in my throat. I closed my eyes as other dancers joined us and floated on a cloud of rosy delight. When the music stopped, I could scarcely keep my feet and he had to steady me with his arms about me.

It was then that I caught a glimpse of Lindsey, and she was deep in conversation with someone I didn't know across the room. I think Gordon saw her too, but neither of us had time to comment on it. I frowned. When had she come in?

I could see she had seen us, and that she would be making her way across the room to us. In that moment, however, Sir Henry, who was standing next to Gordon, turned to the open doors, through which a man in the bright uniform of the maharaja's household burst following the butler, who was making a path to the resident.

Over the din of laughter and voices, a clock chimed the half-hour past midnight, just as the Nepalese came and stood at attention in front of Sir Henry and Gordon. There was hardly a sound as the man spoke in English.

"Sir Lawrence. I make apologies for breaking in on your evening. But you must come. There has been a dreadful tragedy. His Royal Highness is requesting your presence, at the palace." He leaned over and whispered in Sir Henry's ear.

Sir Henry did not show one shred of emotion as he took Gordon's arm and said briefly, "Come with me, Gordon. You'll know what to do. Guggun Singh has just been slain by an unknown assassin, not two hundred yards from the compound, in the temple."

Gordon gave my hand a touch that said everything, and without a word left me to hurry out of the room with Sir Henry and several other men whom the resident called after him. I caught a glimpse of Sir Ralph leaving Jane to follow out, and there was a general hush over all the guests.

So it had happened; the thing which Gordon had somehow feared. Guggun Singh, the Rani's favorite. Had it been done by one of the chief ministers of the King? Everyone began to speculate. Oh, yes, I heard it said, ". . . there will be a retaliation, mark my words!"

I stood beside Lady Jennifer. "Her Royal Highness is a little she-devil in matters like this. She will have revenge, make no mistake. Perhaps we shall all suffer meanwhile." Her words seemed to echo again and again in those next hours, for it was true. No one could leave the compound or come in. It was sealed off as we learned that the palace in Durbar Square was.

It was to be a long wait, and Lady Jennifer decided it was a must for everyone to remain in the party until word came back to us of exactly what had happened. She had card tables set up, and another light refreshment buffet. It was unseemly, however, to have music and dancing, for that would indicate disrespect for the royal household. The very fact that the murder took place just outside the walls of the compound stirred everyone's imagination and brought apprehension to everyone who knew just how the unstable government was toppling.

In all of the hushed speculations, I didn't join in with the group to which Lindsey had attached herself. I knew she must have been told how things had turned out for me and Gordon; there was no question of her not knowing it. And it occurred to me that she would have learned about the presence of Bianca and Toby and Gavin by now.

From where I stood in a cool shadowy corner of the verandah, away from the lights of the room, I could see her standing like a vision of loveliness among her friends. Indeed, she was an attractive woman, and I had little darts of envy stabbing at my heart, for I knew she had been Gordon's mistress, even here in Kathmandu.

The voices came out of the cool darkness behind me out in the garden; I did not even recognize the owners, and I would have moved away had I not heard my own name mentioned.

"It's been one night of surprises, don't you agree?" said a male voice. "I had no idea that Lord Gordon had ditched Lady Lindsey for Gavin Butler's sister. Good Lord, but that is a switch!" and his ebullient chuckle angered me.

"I agree with you, old man," said another male voice. "But Lila here certainly knows a bit of scandal about that strange young woman, don't you, my love?" And I knew it was the voice of Miles Downing, a pompous middle-aged man whose own lust for every woman he saw lighted up his full, florid face.

"It's outrageous the way some women can actually project themselves out into the limelight, and Tawny Butler is one of them," Lila Downing said. "Of course, she was a very young woman at the time, but then . . . well. Lady Lindsey knew her, of course, for she was engaged as a well-paid companion to her husband's younger sister. Mind you, I'd have never thought to hire a woman like Tawny Butler to come into my family, and trusted her as Lady Lindsey did! But she became the mistress of Lady Lindsey's husband."

"No! Can you beat that? And now she steps in and takes Lord Gordon right out from under her very eyes!"

I was frozen to the spot; in front of me, I was staring at Lindsey across the room, caught up in an animated conversation that lit up her whole personality; behind me was the sordid slander which only Lindsey could have made known!

"Well, I have it that it all happened on the caravan which she just happened to have joined in western Nepal. And, can you beat this? She has a baby boy with her, and gave out that she was married to Tobias Roberts, no less, saying the baby was his! But Lady Lindsey knows differently. The baby is none other than Lord Gordon's nephew—that little wayward sister of his who disappeared last year. He will inherit a vast fortune, so it seems, and Miss Tawny Butler will become a very rich woman!"

"Good God! So that's the way the wind blows, is it? I wonder whatever happened to Gavin Butler, and to Tobias Roberts for all that. Something has been going on quite undercover for over a year, and I haven't been able to put my finger on it all. I'd give anything to know . . ."

I moved then. I walked along the verandah until I came to the corner of the house, and it was then I heard a whisper. I turned to see Jaseen's face in the darkness.

"Jaseen!" I reached him, but before I could ask why he had come, he gestured to be quiet. He was pale, and unsmiling.

"You must come. Where Mr. Gordon? Must come quickly."
I heard the desperation in that sentence.

My heart stood still. "Jaseen. What is it? Is Mark—" I didn't
finish my question, for I saw without a doubt that something
had happened to Mark.

"You come, come . . ." and I saw the glimmer of tears in his
own eyes. "Chanda and Mark gone! Someone come, take baby
and Chanda. I not know who, not know when." The words
seemed choked in his throat.

In the next agonizing minutes, Jaseen and I raced back to
Gordon's rooms and found Pemba trembling in fear.

I did not hesitate; I rushed into the reception room, demanded to know which room Tobias Roberts was in, and the
sleepy night clerk had no choice but to tell me. When I
reached his rooms, I knocked loudly, and it was somehow an
eternity before the door opened and Toby stood there, his
beard bright over the kimono he'd thrown around him.

"Tawny! What in God's name—" He saw Jaseen behind
me.

"Toby. I need your help."

I had forgotten that Jaseen had not known of Toby's arrival
and safety, or of my brother and Bianca. So it was a surprise for
him.

"Come in, both of you. Now, tell me what is this all about?"
He had command of the situation, and I blurted out, very
badly, I know, the whole story.

"So, the baby and Chanda are missing?" he said at last. He
had lighted a lamp and we were seated in deep armchairs of
brown leather. "Do Gavin and Bianca know this?"

I shook my head. "No. I came to you first, because I know
she hasn't even seen Mark. And Gordon has gone with Sir
Henry." I told him of the disastrous murder.

"Then we must search the grounds. We'll get a search party
going right now. She can't have gone out of the compound, unless it was before the gates were closed. Now. You sit tight
while I get some clothes on. We'll get this solved before Bianca
knows about it."

By half past two in the morning, Toby had organized a search party that began a fine combing of every inch of the British compound grounds. He was thorough. We had returned to the Lawrence bungalow, and only when I saw the utter surprise in many of the faces there did I realize that Toby and Gavin and Bianca's presence in Kathmandu had been kept a closely guarded secret. Even Lady Jennifer had not revealed their presence.

I would have been in on the search myself, but Toby insisted that I remain in Lady Jennifer's company. And it was agony. Hot coffee was passed around, and Jane came up to me and took my hand. But nothing she could say could dispell the uneasiness that began to take possession of me.

Most of the ladies present were wives and daughters of the men in the British government, and some were with the East India Company. The situation deteriorated badly when no report had come in, and everyone suddenly seemed overtired and irritable, fanning himself, and generally looking like a wilted wallflower.

I became aware of hushed whispers in little groups about the room and on the verandah, where the ladies found their way. And it was then I was conscious of a very strained atmosphere around me. I caught sight of Lindsey, and a horrible sinking feeling swept over me as I saw her walking toward me, her red mouth working strangely.

She came very close to me, and stood over me, so that I would have no chance of escape, as if I had wanted to, and which I did want to before the minute was gone.

"Well, Tawny? What have you to say about all this?" She didn't speak loudly, but in a very calm soft voice, endurance in every syllable. Yet it was loud enough for everyone to turn and listen with sudden and startling sullen faces.

"What are you talking about, Lindsey?" I said, almost breathlessly rude.

"Oh, I'm sure you must know, my dear Tawny! Lady Bianca's baby son has disappeared from his crib . . ."

Nothing could have prepared me for this audacity of hers, so I simply stared at her, trying hard to see where she was leading. That she had already sowed the seeds of malice, I did recall; for Lila Downing stood near Lindsey with a sullen look on her face.

"Just what are you implying, Lindsey Pearson?" I asked.

"As if you didn't know, or shall I tell them?"

"Tell them? And what can you tell them that would not implicate your own dark sins, *dear* Lady Lindsey? Are you willing to risk all on this night of confession?" The dagger I had wanted to use on her had finally been stabbed where it most hurt. She glared at me angrily.

"You are branded as a little hussy! You know how to snatch husbands!" She stopped; her hands had drawn up in knots, and her face became contorted.

"Pray, dear Lindsey!" I said, laughingly. "And, why should I want to take Bianca's baby, when I know she is here to claim him? Explain, if you dare, to these . . . ladies, your own ulterior motives for spreading your malicious slander, but as for me, I will have no more of this confession, which I am certain is causing a great deal of embarrassment for every"—I looked directly at Lila Downing—"no, for almost every lady present."

I stood up and faced her; then, because she stood so close, I gave her a gentle shove aside and strode across the room. It was just as well I did, for at that moment a shout came to us from the doorway.

"They are found! Both the nurse and the baby!"

Everyone turned to stare as Toby entered carrying Mark in his arms, with a bedraggled Chanda trailing after him, Jaseen and other men following, lanterns set aside on the verandah.

"They are both safe, Tawny," Toby said. "And thank God! Chanda is a bit mussed up, I believe. Give her something hot to drink, please." He spoke with full authority to one of the servants standing nearby. Then he handed Mark over to me.

The room behind us seemed to have come to a frozen standstill, and Toby walked inside and stood in front of Lindsey.

"Lady Pearson," he said gruffly. "I believe Chanda has one hell of a story to tell us."

She had blanched white, but her eyes were angry. "I can't think what that would have to do with me. It's Tawny Butler—"

But Chanda, who had come into the room, ran over to Lindsey, and she hissed like a snake, and pointed her finger at Lindsey.

"Bad woman. Take baby. Tie Chanda up." It couldn't have been more dramatic or condemning.

Lindsey, however, chose to deny it strongly. But even as she began to protest, Toby shook his head. "You will have a lot of explaining to do, Lady Lindsey. But we all shall go into this at the proper time. Your rooms have already been confiscated for a search. Don't try to leave the compound. It seems we do have martial law upon us, and I shouldn't vouch for anyone's safety in those streets."

Beyond a doubt, Lindsey had been put in her place, for Toby explained. "We found them both in Lindsey's rooms. Chanda was bound and gagged and thrust behind a sofa. Mark was sleeping peacefully, but locked in a closet. So, dear Lady Lindsey. Behave yourself properly." Someone tittered in the background and I saw that shook her badly, for she began to tremble violently.

"Just who do you think you are, Mr. Roberts? I demand to see Gordon, to tell him the whole truth about . . . you and this little . . . doxy, Tawny—" He reached out and slapped her face with such a blow that it resounded in the room. She gasped, fell back, and then completely broke up. She screamed, demanding to see Gordon, stomping her foot, and only became quiet when Lady Jennifer, at Toby's suggestion, hurried over to her and, with another lady, helped her from the room, assuring Toby that they'd look after her.

It was a traumatic moment for all of us, and I hugged Mark to me, so grateful that he and Chanda were safe, when I realized tears were standing in my eyes.

Toby turned to me. "I'll get you back to Gordon's rooms, Tawny. Let's go now." He was the old loyal Toby, and something stuck in my throat as I followed him with Chanda and Jaseen behind us, down the steps and out into the night.

12

The dawn broke in the east, all crimson and gold over the snow peaks, massive, corrugated, which ringed the Kathmandu Valley. I stood on the verandah outside of Gordon's sitting room, with a cup of steaming coffee in my hands. I had changed from my silk gown into a jade-colored silk kimono, tied around the waist.

Toby stood there with me, quiet in deep study, smoking his comfortable old pipe. The aromatic smoke lifted in the cool still air between us as I turned and found his eyes on me.

"I could have loved you, Tawny," he said quietly. "You know that. But I do not wish to cause pangs of what might have been. Gordon is the fortunate man in this instance, and I do want to let you know I wish you both the best that life together can bring you. Please believe that."

It moved me more than any speech could have done. I couldn't speak for a moment, and when I did, I could only say, "Thank you, dear Toby."

Then he smiled at me in the old familiar way. "We have much to talk over, don't we, my girl?"

"Yes. Yes, we do."

He put his pipe aside and saw Pemba with the pot of coffee. "I'd like a cup of that, my boy," he said. We both leaned back on the verandah rail and sipped the coffee in silence for a small moment; then Toby said, looking up across the steam:

"Have you ever heard of the Jade Pagoda, Tawny?"

I frowned, inclining my head to one side. "Not . . . like that, no." I immediately thought of the two priceless pieces of jade that were made into pagodas, and which I had taken from around my waist not more than two hours ago.

He chuckled. "Well, I daresay, put like that it does sound remote and, quite like some ancient temple, unattainable! But, I am speaking of the name given to certain valuable and priceless Chinese jade pieces, made in the shape of pagodas. There are two of them sitting in locked glass cabinets in the manor hall of the Hardings' Devon home. They belonged to your grandfather, Tawny. He took them back to Butlers Reach, but because of existing debts, Lord Howard Harding claimed them as payment."

I said nothing. I couldn't, for I truly had not known this; but I knew I was tense; what of the two existing jade pagodas which I had carried all the way from Hunza? My heart began to hammer oddly.

"There are two other such objects, Tawny, and it was for these that Khan Shayet murdered David Markus. I myself was baffled to no end when that Kirghiz chief carried out such ruthless measures; in fact, I had no knowledge of these valuable objects until Gavin told me about them. He's been working on this case for several years. For they've been missing links to a chain of smuggling priceless objects from the old palaces of long gone wealthy noblemen throughout China."

"And did Gavin know about the two which our grandfather had smuggled out?" I knew my voice carried all the bitterness that had rankled me over the weight of years and toward the family of Hardings, and in that one sentence, a cloud lifted, and I seemed free.

"Oh, yes. He was keen on discovering where they originated. He asked to be put on this particular case, and Gordon, along with Sir Henry, knew he was just the man for solving it. Everyone suspected Markus and, by gad, he did have them! Gavin was going to meet him; oh, he had a haul of opium in that caravan, but that was just a ploy, and Khan Shayet knew it."

I shivered suddenly. "David gave me one of those pagodas, along with the documents of his marriage to Bianca, Toby. To hand over to Gordon. And Bianca had the other one. She gave it to me, and Khan Shayet pursued me all the way down through Ladakh and Tibet into Nepal because he knew I had them."

It was in that moment we heard the drums begin like the sound of thunder rolling across the city to us. It was startling, for there was no ceasing of it even as we stood up and faced the east, from where it was coming.

"It's in the palace! Something has happened, and it's not good," Toby said in a quiet voice.

We heard the door open from inside and I turned anxiously, desiring to see Gordon, but it was Gavin who rushed inside, sleep still flushing his cheeks. He had dressed hastily and had hurried over from the other wing, where he and Bianca had been given rooms.

At the sight of my brother, my heart dipped into a joy all over again that he was alive and here with me. I ran to him and he hugged me close, burying my head in his chest, while he kissed my forehead gently.

"What the hell's going on here?" he asked over my head at Toby. "Why those drums? Where is Gordon?"

Toby had followed me inside, and he gestured to Pemba to bring hot coffee for Gavin. Then he proceeded to tell Gavin about last night's tragic murder of Guggun Singh in the old temple adjacent to the compound.

"There will be a certain and exact vengeance poured out by Her Royal Highness before this day is out. I fear it's already started."

I moved out of Gavin's arms and gestured for him to sit down, and when the coffee was brought in, I told him of Lindsey's strange abduction of Mark and Chanda and of Toby's solving it. I turned to Toby.

"Why did you say her rooms were confiscated, Toby?"

"Well. It seems she has been opening Gordon's mail, intercepting it before he could know it came. I saw all this from one glance in a desk last night. Believe me. She will have to answer for a lot. Remember those letters I sent out from Gilgit to

Gordon? Well, she intercepted them. So he never even knew about Bianca until you told him, am I right?"

I nodded. "She certainly did know something, and she tried hard to get it from me. Gordon kept her at bay too, by saying that I was married to you, Toby, and that Mark was ours. But she came to me only last evening and said she knew that Mark was Bianca's son. How could she know that? Gordon hadn't told her."

Toby nodded. "Well. I suspect she must have seen the proof, for among those very letters were the marriage documents of Bianca and Markus. That is why I took measures to have her rooms confiscated, locked tight so that she could not destroy evidence." He turned to Gavin, who had been quiet and thoughtful during this talk.

"Gavin, old boy. It seems as if your sister has the same keen spirit that you and your incredible grandfather, Sir James Butler had for the intrigue and adventure of smuggling on the old caravan routes out here! She brought the jade pagodas down from Hunza to Kathmandu, outwitting the old Kirghiz chief himself!" His eyes were full of laughter.

Gavin sat up. "You're joking! Tawny—" He stared at me, his face one of complete surprise.

I stood up, and walked across the room. "Wait here," I said, and I went into the bedroom where Chanda slept soundly with Mark curled into her bosom, and I lifted the petticoats I'd stripped off and removed the leather pouches, and returned to the sitting room.

I handed them over to Gavin. "Didn't Bianca tell you?"

He shook his head. "I didn't ask her. I believed they were lost. I had no idea that you had them." And I told them both how David had given the one to me, and then, later, Bianca had insisted that I bring them down to her brother.

"Gordon wanted me to keep them until we arrived here. He felt sure they were safe with me. I wonder if he suspected that Lindsey searched through his things?"

Neither man looked up at me, but had taken the beautiful glowing jade objects from the pouches and had placed them on a lacquered table in front of them. Then, carefully, they took the objects and twisted their gilt-edged roofs gently, and they opened. Gavin put a handkerchief down on the table and tipped the contents from it, as did Toby. It stunned us all, for a king's ransom of diamonds and emeralds and large glowing rubies fell out.

Gavin laughed. "Well, Tawny? You were just damned lucky that you didn't lose your head for this ransom! What an amazing turn of events! Khan Shayet will be waiting and watching no matter which way we go out, eh, Toby?" He chuckled deeply, then stood up. He stared at me strangely, but I could never have been so proud of such a look.

"What an incredible woman you are!" he finally said.

Toby grinned. "I thought so from the very first, when I saw her there in that lovely old house in Srinagar, Gavin. But she's one of us now."

We heard sounds coming through the grounds, and a thunderous volley of shots resounded through the morning air. Toby jumped up and raced with Gavin out onto the verandah.

"It's from the palace, by gad!" Toby exclaimed. "I'd give a mint to know what's happening. Why the hell doesn't someone let us know?"

The news came not half an hour later.

Gordon returned, his face inscrutable. "They've murdered all the King's ministers in the Kot courtyard," he said, unemotionally. "It was a massacre, and it was done by Her Royal Highness. Her men, including Jung Bahadur and his brothers, hid themselves with weapons, and when the King's men were called to come forward, they had no idea of what had happened, and were innocent victims in their own blood."

It was the beginning of Jung Bahadur Rana's rise to power, and although the Rani had given him the opening for this power, she was not to share it; for within weeks both she and her husband, whom she hated, had to flee their kingdom into exile, and the Rana era began.

*

Gordon and I were married one week later in a beautiful ceremony at the resident's chapel. I believe I could never have been a happier bride, because I had my brother to give me away.

The whole affair of Lindsey's fraudulent life had been exposed; she had been involved with a smuggling team from Calcutta and Delhi when she came out to India; she had gone through Gordon's papers, and to this she broke down and confessed. But Sir Henry, in the aftermath of all the tragedy during those days, felt lenient and let her go free. She left just hours after the closed inquest, rather shamefaced and almost in dishonor.

Both Gavin and Gordon had known about the incident in my past; Father had told Gavin all about it, and Gavin had never implied by word or look that he'd known.

So it all ended happily for me as I walked down the aisle on Gavin's arm, and spoke my vows with the man I loved, then came out into a paradise as his wife.

Bianca, who had been so obviously delighted to reunite herself with her little son, had had a long talk with Gordon. In the end, she gave Gordon and me the right to take him with us to Kashmir to raise in his tender years, because, as she said: "The highroads of China and Tibet are not the place to raise a child. And Gavin and I must be together now. You will both be good for him."

She and Gavin had taken it upon themselves to get the jade pagodas back to where they belonged, and Toby was going with them.

It was an incredible moment for all of us; it was still the old cloak-and-dagger intrigue with my brother, but it all appealed to Bianca, who, I learned, loved and trusted Gavin with a love that seemed more than a love. They seemed separate, and different from other people, sharing a thought together.

I liked the idea, and I knew it would be this way with Gordon and me. Thus we all set forth upon our different adventures on the same day: as Gordon and I started out for Kashmir, taking Mark and Chanda and Jaseen with us, another small caravan began climbing toward the great Himalayas to the north.

"Lady Tawny Harding," whispered my new husband in my ear. "You will have enough adventure from now on just being my wife. Don't you find that intriguing already?"

I looked into his smoke-gray eyes and knew that all of my happiness was in this very promising and real beginning.

"It's the most intriguing moment of my life," I said.

And he leaned over and kissed me gently, as a deep warm joy ran all through me. The future loomed bright, for we were together and we would come back to this lovely old kingdom when spring came around again.